Robert Jackson was born in 1941 and educated at Richmond School, Yorkshire. He has been a full-time author since 1969, specializing in aviation and military history. During his life he has travelled extensively, and speaks five languages; he has flown a wide variety of aircraft, ranging from jets to gliders. He is a recently retired member of the Royal Air Force Volunteer Reserve, and is currently working on the seventh book in the Yeoman series.

# OPERATION DIVER

## Yeoman on Special Missions

### ROBERT JACKSON

**CORGI BOOKS**
A DIVISION OF TRANSWORLD PUBLISHERS LTD

OPERATION DIVER
A CORGI BOOK 0 552 12105 3

Originally published in Great Britain by Arthur Barker Limited

PRINTING HISTORY
Arthur Barker edition published 1981
Corgi edition published 1983

This book is set in 10 pt. Times

Corgi Books are published by Transworld Publishers Ltd.,
Century House, 61-63 Uxbridge Road,
Ealing, London W5 5SA

Printed and bound in Great Britain by
Cox & Wyman Ltd, Reading

# Chapter One

The March wind that came gusting out of the darkness down the valley of the River Authie was bitterly cold. Driving from the south-east, it sent black clouds scudding over the moon and filled the night with rustling movement as it stirred the long grasses and set the branches of trees creaking in unison with one another.

A small group of people—four men and a woman—crouched in the shelter of a small copse that lay on the edge of a broad meadow. All the men were armed, one with a German Schmeisser and the others with British Sten sub-machine guns. Only the woman carried no weapon, although—unknown to her companions—the bulging briefcase she held tightly to her, in addition to the documents it contained, carried enough explosive to blow them all to oblivion if they were overwhelmed by the enemy.

Out in the meadow, invisible in the darkness, stood three more men, a hundred yards apart, their positions marking the points of an imaginary triangle. Each carried a masked lantern, which would be exposed at the appropriate moment for the briefest possible period—just long enough for an incoming aircraft to locate the field and touch down. The pinpricks of light could just as easily bring a German patrol to the location. It was a nerve-racking business, and one fraught with the utmost peril.

One of the men by the copse spoke suddenly, his slow, almost lazy accent that of the province of Languedoc, in southern France.

'I do not think that it will come,' he said. 'It is already long past the appointed time...the wind is too high, and soon it will bring the storm.'

The woman turned to him, reaching out a reassuring hand and placing it on his shoulder.

'Rest easy, Victor,' she murmured. 'It will come. It always comes, even in weather much worse than this.'

She shivered, recalling nightmare hours on a previous occasion, torn by air-sickness in a freezing, lurching cockpit as her pilot rode through turbulent squalls of sleet a few feet above the icy waters of the English Channel.

She was desperately tired. For Julia Connors, alias Madeleine Lefèvre, one-time war correspondent for the *New York Globe* and now a top agent with the highly secret Special Operations Executive, there had been little respite during the past three months. She had worked as a courier between Resistance cells all the way across France, from the Belgian border to the Pyrenees, leading shot-down Allied airmen on the first leg of their journey home; she had briefed and organized other agents whose task it was to keep a continual watch on the German defences of the Atlantic Wall in the sector between Dieppe and Cherbourg.

Then, suddenly, she had been given another assignment: one which, she had been told, was the most important she had so far undertaken. In a crumbling tenement building on the outskirts of Paris, she had made contact with a man who handed her the briefcase she now carried. Inside it, next to the compartment that held the explosive, a fat wad of papers were sealed inside a waterproof pack. She had no idea what the papers were; no questions had been asked, no explanations volunteered. All she knew was that she had to get the documents to London, and that time was vital.

She had no means of knowing that the mysterious documents had travelled a long and dangerous path across Occupied Europe. Three months earlier they had been stolen from Peenemünde, the German secret weapons research establishment on the Baltic coast, by a scientist who, for a variety of reasons, was opposed to the Nazi regime, and had subsequently been smuggled across Germany and into France by members of the communist resistance organization known as Red Orchestra. The fact that the documents had reached SOE at all was something of a miracle, for no love was lost between the Anglo-American organization and the communists; but someone, somewhere down the line, had made the right decision, and it was to be instrumental in saving thousands of lives.

Nor could she know that the papers she carried were the missing link in a chain of events which had baffled and alarmed Allied Intelligence experts for some time. In the early weeks of 1944, as soon as the winter snows had begun to thaw, London had received word from the French Resistance that the Germans were building curious structures at various points along the Pas de Calais under conditions of strict security. Air reconnaissance had already confirmed that the structures appeared to be long, angled ramps, which had one alarming feature in common.

All the ramps located so far were pointing in the direction of London.

Julia Connors had long since ceased to speculate about the contents of the briefcase. All she knew or cared about was that its possession meant a ticket home, if wartime London could be called home, and a few more hours—perhaps days, if they were lucky—snatched with the man she loved. He, too, lived with danger and fear as his constant companions, although in different forms. With a sudden pang, she realized that she might already be too late, that he might have gone from her, his life snuffed out like a candle flame....

A sudden exclamation from Victor jerked her mind mercifully away from morbid thoughts.

'*Ecoute!* I think I hear it!' His head was turned

slightly to one side, his eyes straining to penetrate the darkness.

A moment later Julia also heard it, faintly at first above the wind, then more clearly as it swelled in volume: the drone of an aero-engine. From the direction of the sound it appeared that the pilot was following the line of the river.

The three men positioned in the meadow waited until the last moment, until they were positive that the engine was British—German aero-engines had a quite different and distinctive note—before exposing their lanterns. First one red light, and then all three, cast their glow over the field.

The black-painted Westland Lysander came sliding down over the western boundary, the noise of its engine dying away as the pilot closed the throttle. It touched down with a rumble, settled on its sturdy, spatted undercarriage and rolled quickly to a stop.

Julia and her companions ran out to meet it. Two shadowy figures disembarked and were greeted by the lantern-bearers, who had now extinguished their lights. There were hasty handshakes and farewells and then Julia was scrambling into the cockpit. strapping herself into a seat recently vacated by one of the other passengers. Even before she was settled in the pilot, gauging that plenty of field remained in front of him, was opening the throttle again to send the Lysander thrusting forward over the grass. After an incredibly short take-off run the machine became airborne and the pilot turned steeply over the tree-tops, setting course north-westwards towards the coast.

The Lysander had been on the ground for less than three minutes, which was about the average time it took one of the highly experienced pilots of No. 161 (Special Duties) Squadron to make a pick-up.

The pilots had no idea of the identity of the people they were carrying; the agents were known simply as 'Joes'. In any case, the concentration needed to accomplish a night flight at low level into the heart of enemy territory was such that few pilots had time to worry about anything other than staying alive. Their workload had been high in recent weeks, following a sharp increase in traffic to and from the Continent, and the risks they ran had increased in proportion. The Abwehr, the Germany military intelligence service, had succeeded in making inroads into the ranks of the various resistance movements in Occupied Europe, and aircraft had been lost when, instead of resistance workers, they had been greeted by heavily-armed German troops.

Flak and fighters were becoming a growing problem, too. On more than one occasion recently, a Lysander had only been able to escape thanks to its high manoeuvrability; the pilots had developed tactics that involved putting the aircraft into a deliberate spin, pulling out right on the deck and then entering a series of steep turns that no fighter could hope to match.

So, on this March night in 1944, the Lysander pilot did not trouble himself with idle thoughts about who his passenger might be, or what her mission was. Anyway, the less he knew, the better for all concerned, the only communication between the Lysander's two occupants came when the pilot, safely out over the Channel now, pointed to a pocket on the side of the cockpit; it contained a flask of coffee and a pack of sandwiches, which they shared.

An hour later the Lysander touched down at Tempsford, 161 Squadron's base in Bedfordshire. The weary and thankful pilot watched his passenger climb into a waiting car and disappear into the night, and then dismissed all thoughts of her from his mind. Later, after debriefing and the traditional post-flight meal of bacon and eggs, he went to his room and fell into an exhausted sleep, assisted by the two pills prescribed by the station medical officer which were now an indispensable part of his 25-year-old life.

'OBERKOMMANDO DER LUFTWAFFE—STRENG GEHEIM!' The

words, flanked by the Nazi swastika and surmounted by the German eagle, stood out starkly at the head of every page. Luftwaffe High Command—Top Secret.

The hands of the wall clock in the Air Ministry's Room 512 pointed to 0800. Outside the tall windows, the streets of London were stirring into life.

The Senior Scientist placed his pipe carefully in an ashtray and surveyed the grave faces of the men seated around the big oak table. Some, like himself, were scientists; others were high-ranking RAF officers, the breasts of their blue tunics splashed with the medal ribbons of a bygone war, a war in which—as boys of nineteen or twenty—they had piloted flimsy biplanes against the cream of the Imperial German Flying Corps. Now, in 1944, they directed the lives and destinies of thousands of men as young as they themselves had once been, flying aircraft with performance and striking power undreamed of a quarter of a century earlier.

The Senior Scientist turned to a young man at his elbow:

'Well, Geoffrey,' he said, 'you are the expert in technical German. How soon can a translation of these documents be made ready?'

The young man wrinkled his brow thoughtfully and rolled a pencil between his fingers.

'If I divert the efforts of all my translation team to the job...then I think we can have it completed by this evening. Say seven o'clock. I'm worried about one or two security aspects, though. At least one member of my team does not have a sufficiently high clearance to handle material of this kind.'

'It will be obtained by midday,' the Senior Scientist told him. 'Otherwise, the chap will be off your team immediately. We can't afford to take risks. If news of this business leaked out, the adverse effect on public morale would be incalculable. I am sure that the Prime Minister will agree, when I confront him and the War Cabinet with the facts this evening. The people of London have endured enough; for something like this to threaten them, just when we are gaining the upper hand...' He left the sentence unfinished.

One of the RAF officer's, an air marshal, spoke suddenly.

'We've got a problem on our hands,' he said. 'No one can deny that. But your problem is to find out as much as you can about the working of these infernal things; my business is to stop them, and I'd like to get cracking on some plans right away. It would help, though, if Geoffrey here could refresh our memories about what we know so far—that is to say, what he has gleaned from a preliminary scrutiny of the enemy documents—without going into too much technical detail.'

The Senior Scientist looked slightly annoyed; too much time, he felt, had already been wasted. Nevertheless, the suggestion brought murmurs of assent from several others round the table, so he reluctantly agreed. 'All right, Geoffrey,' he said, adding pointedly: 'For the Air Marshal's benefit.'

The technical translator cleared his throat and consulted his notes. 'Very well, sir. Basically, what we are dealing with is a pilotless bomb—or, more correctly, a small pilotless aircraft with an explosive warhead. The concept is not new; in the 1930s, the Italians experimented with—' He was interrupted by the Senior Scientist, who testily told him to stick to the facts that concerned them here and now. The young man blushed, then continued:

'The weapon developed by the Germans, according to these documents, is extremely simple. It consists of a torpedo-like fuselage, about twenty-five feet long, fitted with stubby, square-cut wings spanning less than eighteen feet. The tail unit is conventional, with tailplane, elevators, fin and rudder. Most of the construction appears to be of wood.'

He peered at his notes again, turning a page.

'The power-plant is really interesting. It is mounted

11

above the aircraft's rear fuselage in a cylindrical tube and is a reaction motor—the nearest I can get to its name in translation is "pulse jet".'

He stretched out a hand and tapped the German documents, which lay on the table in front of him. 'These,' he went on, 'these, which appear to be a fairly detailed technical precis on the German weapon, presumably for the benefit of senior Luftwaffe officers rather than for scientific staff, give details of the pulse jet's development. Personally, I found the whole concept ingenious in its simplicity. Air is forced into the motor through a series of hinged shutters at the front intake and mixed with a finely atomized spray of fuel, the mixture then being ignited by a form of spark plug. The shutters open and close in rapid succession to admit charges of air, so instead of a continuous burning process the engine operates on the principle of a fast chain of low-frequency explosions. After each one, the expanding hot gases are expelled from the rear of the engine, so providing forward thrust.'

'Yes, yes,' said the Air Marshal, waving a hand, 'but how fast will the thing go?'

The translator consulted his papers, hurriedly converting kilometres into miles per hour.

'About four hundred,' he said, 'although I must emphasize that these figures appear to be based on test flight data. In its operational version the weapon may have a higher performance.'

The Air Marshal's face fell. 'Then we're going to be hard put to catch the damned things. The only fighter we've got in service that can match that sort of speed is the Tempest, and so far we've only two squadrons of them. And we're having trouble with their engines.' he added grimly.

The translator looked thoughtful for a moment, then said: 'Well, sir, there might be one thing in our favour. According to this data, the operational ceiling of the weapon is not greater that seven thousand feet. That's well within the range of most of our anti-aircraft guns, isn't it?'

The Air Marshal nodded. 'True. Nevertheless, trying to hit such a small target at speeds of 400 mph or more will present enormous problems. And if the Huns launch swarms of the bloody things at the same time—well then, by God, most of them will get through to London, no matter how good we are.'

'Defending London might not be our only problem, either,' the Senior Scientist interjected quietly. 'According to Geoffrey's notes, these weapons have a range of something like two hundred miles. London lies only half that distance from the enemy launching sites which our air reconnaissance has detected on the other side of the Channel. Furthermore, it seems that the Germans have experimented with launching the bombs from aircraft; if that technique is adopted operationally, no target in the British Isles will be safe.'

'Can the weapon be jammed?' asked an elderly civilian, an electronics expert, who was sitting next to the Air Marshal.

The Senior Scientist shook his head. 'We don't think so. But Geoffrey can explain that more fully.'

'It isn't radio-guided,' the translator said, 'I've seen references here to an Askania gyroscope, which corrects its direction and attitude once it has been launched. Some sort of automatic timing device—I haven't yet had time to work out exactly what kind—cuts out the motor after the weapon has flown the required distance.'

'And then it dives to the ground,' mused the Air Marshal, 'and its ton of high explosive goes off in the middle of London, or wherever the target happens to be.'

He leaned forward suddenly in his seat, his hands clasped together. His mind had been working overtime for the past few minutes, and already he was coming to grips with the problem.

From the little he had heard so far, assuming the technical details were correct—and there was no reason

13

to think that they were not—there appeared to be two ways of stopping one of these infernal devices once it was airborne: either by shooting it down with a direct hit, or by somehow toppling it over—with a near miss from a heavy shell, for example—so that its gyroscope ceased to function and the weapon fell short of its target, with any luck in open country.

He knew, however, that this was not the real answer. The solution was to prevent the new enemy weapons ever getting off the ground by destroying their launching sites. It could be done. A few days earlier, in the middle of March, the combined British and American bomber forces had begun a series of massive attacks against enemy rail centres in northern France in preparation for what everyone in positions of high authority now knew was only weeks away: the Allied invasion of western Europe. Surely some of that awesome striking power, he thought, could be diverted to destroying what might turn out to be the biggest imaginable threat to the success of the invasion.

The Air Marshal tried hard to put himself in the enemy's position. If he had a fleet of long-range pilotless bombs at his disposal, he would not direct them at cities—but at the ports where, very soon, the huge invasion fleets would be massing. The consequences did not bear contemplation.

Back in his office, he at once began to draft a plan for submission to the British Air Staff—a plan outlining firm offensive action that would eradicate the menace of the flying-bombs before it had time to develop fully.

What was it the Germans called the device, with their peculiar sense of devilish drama? Vergeltungswaffe Eins, or something like that. Anyway, it meant 'Reprisal Weapon Number One'—or v-I for short.

The Air Marshal labelled his plan, 'Operation Diver', which seemed appropriate enough—and yet, at the same time, strangely inappropriate for this impersonal, winged torpedo speeding across the sky with a ton of death in its

14

nose and no human hand at its controls. He wondered what other weird devices the German scientists were concocting in their witch's kitchen. There was something sinister about the whole thing; as an Englishman would say, it wasn't cricket.

Suddenly, the Air Marshal chuckled. The overall plan would retain the code-name of Operation Diver: but thoughts of cricket, together with the fact that the v-1s had no pilot, had provided him with a beautifully apt code-word for the missiles themselves. Henceforward, they would be known as 'No-Balls'.

Over the weeks that followed, the very mention of the name would give many Allied pilots nightmares.

# Chapter Two

Flight Lieutenant Steve Hardy, his visage as unsmiling as ever—a trait that had earned him the nickname of 'Happy'—pushed the plate of food away from him and glowered at it distastefully.

'My God,' he complained, 'it gets worse. How the hell you can eat that muck beats me.'

Yeoman looked at his mournful navigator across the breakfast table and grinned.

'Scrambled egg and fried potatoes,' he said, 'make an excellent and very nourishing breakfast dish. Go on, get it down your neck.'

'No thanks,' grunted Hardy. 'I'll just have a bit of toast.'

'In that case,' Yeoman said, reaching out for Hardy's plate and forking its contents on to his own, 'I'll have yours. It's delicious, especially the burnt bits. In any case,' he added, 'you're getting too fat.'

'Which is surprising, considering he's been slowly shagging himself to death for weeks now.' Hardy's liaison with a little WAAF section officer from Group HQ was well known to his colleagues, who ribbed him unmercifully at every opportunity.

Hardy glared at the man on his left, Flying Officer Terry Saint, who had just spoken.

'Your New Zealand twang, or drawl, or whatever the hell you choose to call it, grates on my nerves at this time of morning,' he said. 'It's too early for your brand of humour.'

He rose from the table and pushed his chair into place. As he turned to leave, Saint said:

'Hey, have you heard about Snow White's dwarfs, all sitting in the bath and feeling happy?'

'What?'

'Happy got out!'

Yeoman spluttered helplessly, choked on a mouthful of potato and turned red in the face. Hardy moved round the end of the table and pounded him hard on the back before disappearing in the direction of the anteroom, picking up a fresh cup of tea en route.

'He smiled,' Saint observed with mock amazement. 'I'll swear he smiled.'

'Highly unlikely,' commented Yeoman. He finished his—or rather Hardy's—egg and potato and began to spread margarine and jam on a thick slice of bread. Saint looked at him and shook his head slowly.

'I don't know how you do it, boss,' he said. 'I honestly don't know how you do it.'

Yeoman wagged a finger at him. 'The secret of a healthy life and regular habits,' he explained, 'is to have a good breakfast. It doesn't matter what else you eat, as long as you get some food inside yourself at the start of the day. It gets the system going.'

He finished his bread and jam and drained his teacup, looking at his watch.

'Right,' he said, 'there's still an hour before pilots' briefing. Come on, we might as well catch the news.'

They went into the anteroom together and found that someone had already switched on the radio. A few aircrew, all of them members of 380 Squadron, which Yeoman commanded, were slumped in armchairs reading the papers, which had just arrived. Yeoman picked up a copy of the *Daily Mail* and glanced at the headlines: the Russians were closing in on Odessa, the Prime Minister was at Harrogate attending a civic reception, documents captured by the Royal Ulster Constabulary allegedly showed that the Irish Republican Army was planning to co-operate with the enemy, and British fighters from an aircraft carrier had shot down an American transport aircraft over the Atlantic, mistaking it for a German Focke-Wulf Condor reconnaissance plane.

Yeoman read the last report with interest, for he had always felt the need for accurate and fast aircraft recognition. The report mentioned that the American aircraft had apparently approached an Allied convoy, which the British naval fighters were defending, without giving the appropriate recognition signals, but to his mind this was no excuse for precipitating a tragedy. He imagined that the American transport must have been a Douglas C-54 which, he was forced to admit, bore an uncanny resemblance to the Focke-Wulf aircraft from certain angles, and since the presence of a Condor near a convoy meant that a U-boat pack was in the offing, the fighter pilots must have been understandably trigger-happy.

Yeoman laid his newspaper aside as the deep, cultured tones of the BBC newsreader came over the air.

'In the early hours of this morning, a large force of Lancasters and Halifaxes of RAF Bomber Command carried out a saturation attack on the Nazi rally city and industrial centre of Nuremberg. According to an Air Ministry communiqué released a little under an hour ago, ninety-four of our bombers failed to return.'

In the brief pause that followed this fearful announcement, there was a stunned silence in the anteroom. All faces were turned towards the radio, as though willing the announcer to retract the figure he had just given. Quietly, someone said: 'Jesus Christ!'

Remorselessly, his voice sombre, the newsreader went on:

For most of their journey, the bombers had to battle their way through determined fighter opposition. Returning crews said that the enemy have made no greater effort to save one of their cities, not even Berlin. Although it was cloudy over most of the route, there were many clear patches with bright moonlight both on the way to the city and back.

'The attack began a little after one o'clock in the

morning, and the moon did not set until two. The bitterest fighting ever known since the Battle of Germany began took place while the moon lasted, and this was for two hours out of the three spent over enemy territory. Fighter packs were brought up as soon as the bombers crossed the enemy coast, and as the bombers penetrated further inland all the ground defences joined in. Vapour trails gave away the position of some of the bombers when they encountered unexpected freezing conditions at medium altitudes.

'This is the biggest loss ever suffered by the RAF in a single assault....'

The announcer moved on to other topics. Hardy suddenly swore, got up and switched off the radio.

'Ninety-four...' Terry Saint muttered. 'God, I've never heard anything like it. They must have got the figures wrong.'

Yeoman shook his head. 'No, the figures will be right enough. If anything, they'll be underestimated. I don't understand how it can have happened, though.'

'It happened because somebody made an almighty cock-up, that's how!'

The bitter voice made them all turn sharply towards the door of the anteroom. The man who stood there was big, over six feet tall, with the broad shoulders and bull neck of a rugby forward. He wore a squadron leader's rank braid, and the row of medal ribbons under his pilot's wings included the Distinguished Flying Cross. His face was pale and drawn, his fists clenched in suppressed anger.

Yeoman had never seen Squadron Leader Clive Bowen, CO of 373 Squadron, in such a state of tension before; the big Welshman was usually soft-spoken and calm, as steady as a rock in any circumstance. Yeoman knew, however, that the Mosquito night fighters of No. 373, which shared RAF Burningham in Norfolk with his own squadron, had been out for most of the night over the Low Countries and Germany, operating in support of

19

Bomber Command. It must really have been a nightmare out there, to produce this kind of reaction.

'Hello, Clive,' he said, as casually as possible, 'come and join us. I thought you'd still be asleep.'

Bowen slumped wearily into an armchair next to Yeoman and passed a hand over his eyes.

'Sleep,' he murmured. 'Yes, I reckon I could do with a few hours. Later, maybe. Just now, I feel I could do with some tea. Wish there was some coffee.'

'Rough night?' Yeoman enquired.

'God, yes, George. We saw them falling out of the sky all the way from the Dutch coast, one after another. It was sheer bloody murder, just as if the Huns knew we were coming.'

He stared suddenly at Yeoman, his eyes haunted.

'Maybe they did know, at that,' he said. 'Half-way over the North Sea my navigator and I were both convinced that we heard a transmission on the command guard frequency from one of our own aircraft. It was just a short burst of R/T, as if somebody had been talking to his crew over the intercom and had pressed the transmit button by mistake as he was in midsentence, but I'll swear the word "Nuremberg" was mentioned. It can't have been a figment of the imagination, not when we both thought we'd heard the same thing. And if we heard it, you can bet your boots the Huns did too.'

Terry Saint, who had temporarily left the anteroom, now returned with a large cup of tea, which he handed to Bowen. The latter took it and nodded his thanks, smiling thinly. Then, turning back to Yeoman, he went on:

'You know, George, some bastard on the planning staff ought to have his neck wrung. From Charleroi, the bomber stream was routed direct to Fulda—straight past two fighter assembly beacons. I think that was where they took their biggest losses. We saw the poor buggers going down in flames all over the place, and the sky was stiff with fighter flares.'

He gave a sudden, savage grin. 'At least the sods

didn't have it all thir own way. Jimmy Collins'—he named one of the pilots on his squadron—'Jimmy Collins was patrolling over Beacon Ida, near Aachen, and he got three of 'em in just about as many minutes. All single-engine jobs. They were using a lot of day fighters, George, attacking by the light of the flares. Not that they needed the flares; you could see the bombers from miles away, pulling great brilliant contrails in the moonlight. Bloody picturesque, it was,' he said bitterly.

Yeoman started to ask a question but was interrupted by the crackle of the tannoy on the anteroom wall above the door.

'Squadron Leader Yeoman, telephone,' it said metallically. 'Squadron Leader Yeoman, telephone please.'

He excused himself and went along the corridor to the little alcove that served as the officers' mess reception, where a sleepy aircraftman handed the phone to him across the desk.

The clipped voice on the other end of the line belonged to Group Captain Hector Davison, the Officer Commanding RAF Station Burningham.

'George, can you come down to my office at once?'

'All right, sir. But there's a captains' briefing in thirty minutes.'

'Forget that,' Davison told him. 'It's all been changed.' There was a click, and the line went dead.

Yeoman went to the cloakroom and took his cap from the peg marked OC 380 Sqn, then as an afterthought returned for his greatcoat, for an earlier glance out of his bedroom window had told him that the morning was raw and cold, with a chill mist drifting over Burningham from Methwold Fens.

He went outside and set out on a brisk two hundred yard walk to station headquarters, the frigid air stinging his freshly-shaven face. As he walked, he realized with a sudden shock that it was now almost a year since he had taken command of 380 Squadron; a year that had seen the squadron grow in stature and experience until it was

21

now one of the foremost units of its kind in the RAF.

The squadron was equipped with fast de Havilland Mosquito Mk VIS, formidably armed with four 20-mm cannon and four .303 machine-guns. When operational circumstances required it, they could also carry a pair of 500-lb bombs in the rear of the bomb-bay, a useful addition when carrying out attacks on enemy airfields.

Together, 380 Squadron and the radar-equipped Mosquito night fighters of Clive Bowen's No. 373 formed what was know as the Burningham Wing. This, in turn, was part of No. 100 Group, an élite formation whose task was to support the RAF's night bombing offensive by sowing confusion among the enemy defences and whose motto, appropriately, was 'Confound and Destroy'. From relatively small beginnings in the autumn of 1943, No. 100 Group had grown to a strength of twelve operational squadrons, not counting the Bomber Support Development Unit at Foulsham in Norfolk and one or two small specialist flights. Three of the squadrons—Nos 192, 199 and 214—were equipped with four-engined heavy bombers such as the Short Stirling, Handley Page Halifax or the American-built Boeing Fortress, all of which carried radio countermeasures equipment instead of bombs; their task was to jam the radars that directed the German night fighters. It was a highly dangerous job, for it involved circling over enemy territory in the target area for lengthy periods—and the Germans had now developed equipment that enabled their fighters to home on to some of the countermeasures radar carried by the jamming aircraft.

The other squadrons in the Group were equipped with Mosquitos. Most of them were intruders, their mission to range far and wide over Germany and Occupied Europe under cover of darkness, either swooping down to strike at enemy airfields or patrolling the German fighter assembly beacons in search of worthwhile targets.

380 Squadron, on the other hand, was a day fighter-bomber unit. Its Mosquitos were not fitted with radar;

their role was to carry out pinpoint precision attacks against targets within the German air defence framework—airfields and radar stations, for example—which were held by British Intelligence to be of particular importance.

It could be a costly business. On one fearful day in December 1943, during an attack on the airfield at Bad Zwischenahn, where the Germans were testing new and secret rocket fighters, the squadron had lost eight out of sixteen Mosquitos.

That had been the worst day of all; but this was war, and there had been no time to dwell on losses, however tragic. Under Yeoman's leadership the survivors had welded together the nucleus of a new 380 Squadron, a nucleus of wise, battle-hardened veterans who were examples in every way to the young men who came to replace those who had been lost.

Yeoman thought of them with great affection. Flight Lieutenants Rory McManners and Tim Sloane, his flight commanders, were directly under him in the chain of command; he would lose them both soon, for they had only a few sorties left to fly before their operational tours expired. Terry Saint was in line to replace one of them, while the other's place would eventually be taken by Captain Yves Romilly of the Free French Air Force.

Of the original team which had formed 380 Squadron back in the spring of 1943, only one other pilot, South African Flight Sergeant Chris Lorrimer, remained. Three others—Warrant Officer Arthur Laurie, a Canadian, and two Sergeant Pilots named Hudson and Carr—had joined the squadron later, and had survived the Zwischenahn attack. All the others were newcomers, posted in January 1944 to make good the losses.

That fateful December day had also left Burningham without a wing commander, for the previous one, Charles Rothbury, had been shot down and taken prisoner. The new man, Bentley, had been a single-seat pilot, having flown Gladiators and Hurricanes in the Middle

East and later commanded a squadron of Hawker Typhoons. There was a certain amount of friction between Bentley and Yeoman, but for the life of him Yeoman could not account for it. It was nothing as strong as mutual dislike: in fact, there were times when Yeoman even enjoyed Bentley's company over a game of darts and a pint of beer in the mess. Perhaps, Yeoman thought, it was nothing more than a subconccious childish resentment that he himself had not been given command of the wing.

He reached station headquarters and went inside, treading the well-worn path along the corridor that lead to the CO's office. He had to pass through the adjutant's office first; the adjutant, Flight Lieutenant Rees, had not yet come on duty, but his deputy, a formidable Flight Sergeant, knocked on Davison's door and announced Yeoman's arrival.

On entering, Yeoman had the incredible feeling that he had suddenly been flung back in time. The scene in the office was almost exactly the same as that which had confronted him eight months earlier, on the morning when—on its return from an armament practice camp—380 Squadron had been declared fully operational. Group Captain Hector Davison, DSO ,MC, was seated behind his desk, his eyes as steely as ever over the top of his half-moon glasses, while the man who sat in an armchair opposite, a teacup raised to his lips, had also been present on that other occasion.

'Good morning, George,' Davison said in that clipped voice of his. 'You remember Air Commodore Sampson?'

'Indeed I do, sir,' Yeoman replied, shaking the senior officer's hand. On his last visit to Burningham, Sampson had been a group captain. Promotion prospects must be good in the Air Ministry's Directorate of Operations, thought Yeoman, for Sampson was still in his thirties. Nevertheless, the man had a distinguished career behind him, and he wore the ribbon of the VC, awarded for leading a virtual suicide attack in a Blenheim bomber in daylight earlier in the war.

24

'Well, Yeoman,' the Air Commodore said, 'your squadron has been doing quite well for itself, by all accounts.'

'Thank you, sir,' the younger man answered. 'We like to think so.'

'Yes. Well, we've got another job for you, The whole squadron, I mean.'

He set aside his cup and waved his hand at another armchair, indicating that Yeoman should sit down. In ordinary circumstances, Wing Commander Bentley would also have been present at this meeting, but he was away on leave. Yeoman was secretly pleased.

'First of all,' Sampson went on, 'I have to tell you that you will shortly be leaving 100 Group. In a few days' time you will be leaving for Tangmere to join 83 Group, which as you know is part of the Second Tactical Air Force—the spearhead of the Allied Expeditionary Air Force.'

Sampson saw the look on Yeoman's face and smiled. 'Yes,' he said quietly, 'the invasion is coming. Sooner, perhaps, than a lot of people think. I can't say when or where, for obvious reasons, but we are just about ready. And when it happens, the task of 83 Group will be to secure air superiority over the beaches.'

The Air Commodore's expression grew serious. He took a cigarette from a silver case and lit it, exhaling the smoke in a long stream.

'We are, however, concerned with an immediate problem. We think—in fact, we know—that the Germans have a secret weapon which, if they use it in the right manner could destroy our chances of launching a successful assault on the coast of France.'

He reached down into a briefcase that rested by the side of his chair and extracted a folder, which he handed to Yeoman.

'Take a look at that,' he said. 'Tell me what you think. You have some knowledge of German, don't you?'

Yeoman nodded, a little startled, and opened the folder. For the next few minutes he sat engrossed, taking in the known details of the weapon the Germans called the v-1, poring over the reconnaissance photographs of its launch sites. Finally, he closed the folder carefully and handed it back to Sampson.

'It's incredible,' he said. 'Absolutely astonishing! Do we have a defence against these things, sir?'

Sampson looked at him. 'Oh, we'll doubtless be able to shoot some of them down. The real defence, however, is to hit their launching sites as hard as we can. The trouble is that the sites are absolutely stiff with flak; some sorties have already been flown against them by the medium bombers of 2 Group, and they have suffered considerable losses. So we have been forced to revise our tactics.'

The Air Commodore paused, lit another cigarette, and then continued: 'At this moment, four of 83 Group's Spitfire squadrons are being modified to carry 500-lb bombs and sent across to Llanbedr on the North Wales coast for dive-bombing trials.'

Yeoman shuddered inwardly. The thought of the graceful Spitfire's outline marred by a bomb slung under its belly was almost too much to bear. And as for the idea of using the thoroughbred fighter as a dive-bomber...

'I know what you're thinking,' Sampson said, 'but we've really got no alternative. The sites are much too small for night attacks to have any real hope of success, and as I've said the medium day bombers are suffering too heavily. At least the Spits, with their high speed, will have a good chance of coming through the flak.'

The Air Commodore looked hard at Yeoman. 'However,' he went on, 'not all the sites will be vulnerable to dive-bombing. At least one that we know of is built into the side of a cliff; the Germans are using a series of caves and tunnels near the River Oise to stockpile their pilotless bombs, and they are protected by a roof of earth and rock at least thirty feet thick. The only hope of knocking out this kind of objective is to

26

bounce bombs into the tunnel mouths, and that is where 380 Squadron comes in.'

There was a sinking feeling in the pit of Yeoman's stomach. During their series of attacks on enemy airfields in 1943, he and his pilots had evolved low-level tactics whereby the Mosquitos released their bombs at high speed, a few feet above the ground, and literally skipped the missiles through the doors of hangars. The technique had proved very successful, if dangerous, but so far they had not tried it out against any other type of target.

It looked as if they were now going to have their chance to do so.

'Can it be done?' Sampson asked.

Yeoman, in reply, made little attempt to keep the sarcasm out of his voice.

'Oh, yes, sir, it can be done all right. Provided, of course, that a certain number of conditions are fulfilled.' He ticked them off, one by one, on his fingers.

'First, that we have a straight run-up to the target. Second, that the mouth of our cave or tunnel is big enough. Third, that we can get close enough to bounce our bombs inside without splashing ourselves all over the cliff face. And fourth, that nothing is shooting back at us.'

The air commodore looked at Yeoman for a long moment, his face impassive. Then he said:

'All right, Yeoman, I know how you feel. I know, too, that we seem to be asking the impossible. But it's vital— more vital than you can possibly realize at this point. Otherwise we wouldn't ask in the first place. Now, I'll repeat my question. Can it be done?'

'Probably,' Yeoman said.

Sampson gave one of his thin smiles. 'That's good enough for now. You'll be getting full target data in a day or two.'

He stood up abruptly, as though to close the meeting. He stood a good head taller than Yeoman; the latter had not realized how tall the Air Commodore was.

'There's just one more thing,' Sampson said. 'We want you to be ready to go in two weeks, so it's going to mean a lot of hard work for you and your crews. In the meantime, another daylight bomber "show" against the No-Ball sites is scheduled for next Monday, weather permitting, and the Newchurch Wing will be providing fighter cover. So why don't you nip down there, borrow a Spitfire and take a look at things first hand? The experience might be useful. I'll fix things up, if that's all right with Group Captain Davison.'

'Certainly,' Davison agreed, speaking for the first time. 'And, George—you might be interested to know that one of the Spitfire units at Newchurch is 505 Squadron. You were with them in 1940, weren't you? Might see one or two old faces.'

I doubt it, thought Yeoman, as he saluted and left the office. Most of the old faces I knew from those days are dead. So far, he had been one of the lucky ones; but he had an unpleasant feeling that his luck was about to run out.

# Chapter Three

It was good to be in the cockpit of a spitfire again, even if that cockpit seemed small and cramped in comparison with a Mosquito's.

Yeoman was pleased that he had not lost his old touch; the Spitfire responded to the pressure of his hand on the stick like the thoroughbred she was, riding the currents of air smoothly and effortlessly.

Yeoman had not flown a Spitfire since 1942, when he was in Malta, and that had been an elderly and war-weary Mk v. His present mount was a far different aircraft—a Mk xiv, packed with the power of a big Rolls-Royce Griffon engine, developed from the faithful Merlin, that could thrust it through the sky at a top speed of over 430 mph and take it to an altitude of 43,000 feet. It was armed with two 20-mm Hispano cannon and four .303 machine-guns; it also had a new type of 'tear-drop' cockpit canopy which, unobstructed by metal struts, gave the pilot an unparalleled all-round field of view.

His elevated position under the clear cockpit hood had made Yeoman feel a little exposed at first, but the feeling had passed in minutes and now he sat there and rejoiced behind the whirling arc of the big five-blade Rotol propeller.

He had been right; there had been no familiar faces. The personnel of 505 Squadron had changed continuously since those hectic days of 1940, when its pilots had fought against hopeless odds in the summer skies of France and England. The men who had flown by his side were gone, either sacrificed in battle or scattered to the four winds. He no longer felt a sense of belonging, of identity, and it saddened him; for it was with this squadron that he had learned the tricks of his trade, surviving to become a veteran.

It was the morning of Monday, 3 April, and Yeoman had been at Newchurch—an advanced fighter airfield in Romney Marsh, Kent, close to the Channel coast—for twenty-four hours, having been flown down from Burningham by Terry Saint in the Airspeed Oxford that was used as the station 'hack'.

After a few circuits in the Spitfire xIV to get his hand in once more, he had been shown round Newchurch by Squadron Leader Tim Phelan, a genial Irishman from County Wicklow who was 505 Squadron's present commander. Phelan, a Spitfire man to his fingertips, had come to the squadron from the Vickers factory at Castle Bromwich, where he had spent a year as a production test pilot. As he was nursing a broken wrist, having fallen off his bicycle during the blackout, he offered Yeoman the leadership of the squadron during the forthcoming operation against the No-Ball site, subject to the approval of the Wing Leader. Yeoman jumped at the chance.

505 Squadron shared Newchurch with the Spitfire 9s of No. 56 and the Hawker Tempest 5s of Nos 3 and 486 Squadrons, the latter a Royal New Zealand Air Force unit. Yeoman was particularly interested in the big, powerful Tempests, with their Napier Sabre engines air-cooled through a huge radiator under the nose similar to that of the Typhoon, from which they had been developed; it was the first time he had seen this, the fastest fighter in RAF service, at close quarters. When he expressed interest in flying one he was told that he would have to get in some time on the Typhoon first.

Unlike Yeoman, Phelan treated the Tempest with magnificent contempt.

'Horrible bloody thing,' he snorted. 'Seven tons of

sheer brute force. No fun in flying those, George; steer clear of 'em. I saw one go straight into the deck the other day; some bloke was doing an air test over the field and he pulled too much 'g' in a turn. The Tempest went straight over on its back and flicked into a spin. And that was that. Wham!'

He made an expressive downward gesture with his hand.

'You can't spin 'em, you see, George. It takes thousands and thousands of feet before they'll come out. In fact, one of the 3 Squadron types told me the other day that if you accidentally get into a spin below ten thousand feet, the only thing to do is bale out, fast.'

Yeoman thought that Phelan was perhaps being a little unjust in his attitude to what appeared in most respects to be a superb fighting machine, but made no comment. He resolved to try a Tempest for himself at the first available opportunity.

Nevertheless, as he climbed out over the Channel on this clear April morning at the head of 505 Squadron, he could understand Phelan's sentiments very well. A love affair with the Spitfire was difficult, if not impossible, to break off.

He took the formation up to twelve thousand feet, heading for the cliffs of Cap Gris Nez. Five thousand feet lower down flew the bombers—fifteen North American B-25 Mitchells, fast twin-engined aircraft which were now replacing the ageing Douglas Bostons in the medium bomber squadrons of the RAF's No. 2 Group. Almost exactly two years earlier, an American Major named Jimmy Doolittle had led a formation of Mitchells in an astonishing attack on Tokyo after taking off from an aircraft carrier in the Pacific. They had been the bomber's combat début; now it was one of the most widely-used aircraft of its kind in every theatre of war.

Flak rose to meet them as they crossed the coast, exploding in white puffs around the bombers, but they sailed through it unharmed, their formation as impeccable as ever, So far, there was no sign of any fighters.

The target lay twenty miles inland, in forested country not far from the ancient battleground of Crécy. The Mitchells made for it in an arrow-straight line, their shadows following them, leaping hazily across wooded hillsides and the white-walled hamlets that nestled in their folds.

Yeoman brought the squadron down a couple of thousand feet and warned the pilots to keep their eyes open, but apart from a few streaks of high cirrus cloud the sky remained empty. He turned his attention back to the bombers; they should be just about over the target now, although try as he might Yeoman could not distinguish anything unusual among the green and brown hues of the landscape.

Then the flak came up. Just a few clusters at first, bursting across the path of the bombers, indicating range and altitude to other batteries that lay hidden in the woods. Suddenly, the sky was filled with drifting clouds of smoke as the burst of hundreds of shells speckled the air. It was incredible that anything could survive the holocaust, and yet the Mitchells flew on steadily, straight and level. Yeoman could imagine only too well how the pilots must be sweating with fear and tension as they rode the shock-waves from the shells, waiting for the merciful moment of bomb release.

Each Mitchell carried three thousand pounds of bombs. On a signal from the lead aircraft, twenty tons of high explosive fell from the bellies of the fifteen bombers and plummeted towards the woods. Yeoman saw the explosions ripple across the ground, misty shock waves flickering outwards from them. Light green patches appeared instantly against the darker background as trees crumpled and collapsed in splintered ruin. Dark smoke fountained up, blotting out a rectangular area of woodland.

Two immense flashes glowed vividly through it. Black clouds burgeoned up through the smoke of the bombs, boiling, flameshot pillars that rose to a height of several thousand feet with incredible speed.

The flak continued to rise, thicker than ever, vengefully pursuing the Mitchells as they began a slow turn towards the west, clearing the target area. The Spitfires turned with them, maintaining their higher altitude, and as they did so Yeoman suddenly saw one of the bombers drop slowly out of formation, trailing an intermittent stream of smoke from one engine. Two parachutes popped open in its wake, and an instant later the Mitchell fell into a tight spiral dive. It vanished among the trees in a splash of flame.

The two formations, fighters and bombers, headed flat out for the coast. Suddenly, after five minutes, one of Yeoman's pilots called exciteldy over the R/T:

'One-oh-nine, three o'clock low!'

Yeoman dropped his Spitfire's wing and saw the enemy aircraft almost immediately, flying on a parallel course at about five thousand feet. He pressed the transmit button.

'Roger. Next time, whoever called, identify yourself. Yellow Section, go and get that Hun. The rest of you watch out—there may be others.'

The three Spitfires of Yellow Section peeled off one after the other and dived towards their target. The remainder had a grandstand view as they massacred the unfortunate Messerschmitt, whose mangled wreckage was soon blazing fiercely in a field.

Yellow Section climbed back up to rejoin the formation.

'Must have been blind as a bat,' someone commented laconically.

Three more enemy fighters, Focke-Wulf 190s this time, were sighted near the coast. They followed the British aircraft for some distance, but made no move to attack. Eventually, they turned away.

Times had changed, thought Yeoman. The Luftwaffe's fighter pilots were no longer the aggressive, cocksure men they had been when he had first encountered them, four years earlier; the air war had taken its toll, in morale as well as in human life.

Yet, he thought grimly, it was dangerous to generalize. Some Luftwaffe fighter units were very, very good indeed, and were led by determined men who had been in the war right from the start. Some of them claimed to have shot down formidable numbers of enemy aircraft, particularly on the Russian Front. The Allied air forces might be slowly gaining the upper hand, but the Luftwaffe was far from beaten. Grim days still lay ahead.

The Spitfires accompanied the Mitchells as far as Beachy Head and then the two formations parted company, the bombers turning west towards their base at Hartford Bridge and the fighters heading in the opposite direction towards Newchurch.

They arrived over the airfield to find the circuit crammed with American Mustang fighters, all jockeying for position to land. Yeoman called up Flying Control to find out what was going on and was told that the Mustangs had been out on a big 'show' over Germany, escorting Flying Fortresses on a mission to Magdeburg. Short of fuel, they had headed for the nearest English airfield as soon as they had crossed the coast.

Yeoman managed to find a gap in the middle of all the confusion and slotted his Spitfires into it quickly, bringing them down to land in pairs. He taxied in, weaving carefully between parked Mustangs, and shut down the engine, thankfully freeing himself from the constriction of his seat and parachute harness.

Tim Phelan was waiting for him as he climbed out of the cockpit and jumped down off the wing.

'Well, George. How did it go?'

'One bomber down, one 109 down. Caught him napping. No opposition, except from the flak, and there was plenty of that. Those bomber boys were right on the ball, though; they really plastered the target.'

Phelan nodded. 'They usually do. Trouble is, those

34

bloody No-Ball sites are so hard to find.'

He waved a hand at the conglomeration of American fighters.

'Proper bloody shambles, this is. I hate to think what would happen if the Jerries sent over a few fighter-bombers during the next couple of hours. Come on, let's have a word with the Intelligence Officer and then have a beer or two with the lads before lunch.'

The bar of the officers' mess was packed with Americans, gesticulating and talking in loud voices about the morning's operation. A handful of RAF officers, sandwiched into corners, regarded this alien invasion of their sanctum with expressions closely akin to horror.

Yeoman and Phelan forced their way through the throng to a small oasis that had been formed at one end of the bar by a group of 56 Squadron pilots, who obligingly made way for them and then closed ranks again, determined that not even the full weight of the USAAF fighter group was going to budge them from their position.

Phelan managed to catch the eye of the harrassed barman, obtained their drinks and handed one to Yeoman. The latter took a long swallow, sighed appreciatively and lifted his glass, eyeing what remained of its contents.

'Not bad,' he said. 'Better than average, in fact.'

Phelan grunted. 'Witch's piss. You can't get a good drink this side of Dublin. The English never could make a decent brew.'

The two men launched into a friendly argument on the merits, or otherwise, of English beer. Suddenly, Yeoman started as a loud shout cut through the hubbub of voices in the bar.

'George! George Yeoman!'

The bellow brought a momentary silence. Yeoman swung round, his back to the bar, and his face lit up in a huge grin as he immediately recognized the tall, lanky figure making his way towards him through the crowd of

American pilots, who parted respectfully to let him pass.

A moment later, Yeoman's hand was being pumped vigorously and he was subjected to a series of rib-shaking slaps on the back. Disentangling himself, he said weakly to Phelan:

'Tim, I'd like you to meet an old friend of mine. We were in France together. Lieutenant-Colonel Jim Callender.'

The big American and the Irishman shook hands, then Callender turned to the other Americans, most of whom were pilots in the fighter group he commanded.

'Listen, you guys,' he roared, 'you're all going to have a drink on me! This here's my old buddy, Squadron Leader George Yeoman, and we were kicking shit out of the Krauts while you were still in nappies.'

He turned back to Yeoman, who was feeling faintly embaraassed, and lowered his voice.

'Hey, it's really good to see you, George. I often think about the old days. We had some really good times, then. You know, I pulled every possible string to try and stay with the RAF, but nothing worked.'

Like Yeoman. Jim Callender had flown and fought with 505 Squadron in the early months of the war, having made his way to England via Canada. Later, he had risen to command an 'Eagle' squadron, composed of American volunteers who had enlisted in the Royal Air Force in Britain's hour of greatest peril, long before the entry of Russia and the United States into the war, when the island stood alone against the seemingly invincible might of the Axis.

As the American war effort got under way in the summer of 1942, those responsible for building up the 8th United States Army Air Force in Britain had not been slow to realize Callender's worth as a fighter leader, and had formerly requested his transfer. After a lengthy battle, the USAAF had won and Callender had changed uniforms, although he still proudly wore his RAF pilot's brevet on his tunic opposite the silver wings of the Army Air Force.

'The last I heard of you, you were flying Thunderbolts,' Yeoman said. 'How do you like the Mustang?'

'She's a real honey, George,' Callender enthused. 'She'll do over four hundred miles per hour at 25,000 feet, and she's got a maximum range of two thousand miles. That's the important bit. It means that wherever the bombers go, we can go too. The Hun fighters don't have it all their own way any more, believe me.'

'I believe you, all right' Yeoman said. 'As you know, I was always sceptical about the chances of daylight bombing, but if you can go all the way to the target with the bombers then that's a different story.'

Callender nodded, then grinned his old infectious grin. 'It just so happens that we're the top-scoring Mustang group in the 8th Air Force,' he said. 'I've got six Huns myself since we re-equipped with the little beauties, and that brings my own score up to nineteen. How about you?'

'Twenty-four,' Yeoman answered modestly.

'Jeez!' The comment came from a young American lieutenant, one of a number of pilots who had gradually drifted over and had been listening to the conversation between Yeoman and Callender with interest.

'That's more than our top guys have got,' the lieutenant said.

'Well,' smiled Yeoman, 'you've got to remember that I've been in the war a bit longer!'

The lieutenant continued to gaze at Yeoman in awe, as though he were a creature from another planet. Yeoman was beginning to feel distinctly uncomfortable, like an exhibit in a zoo, when the American's face suddenly crumpled in a frown.

'Say,' he said, 'with all those kills, how come you've only got three medals?'

'Well,' Yeoman replied rather lamely, 'that's just the way we do things in the RAF.'

Callender laughed and addressed the lieutenant. 'The squadron leader had to work pretty hard to earn those medals, son,' he pointed out. 'Look, see that one? That's the Distinguished Flying Medal, which they gave him for leading the retreat to Dunkirk. The next one's the Distinguished Flying Cross, which he was awarded for having the biggest harem in Cairo when he was out in the desert. Actually, the little rosette in the middle means that he was awarded it twice, which accounts for his haggard appearance. And this third one here, which is a Polish medal, he won't talk about, but I can tell you that he came back from his attachment to a Polish squadron smelling of cheap perfume.' He closed one eye in a slow-motion wink.

Yeoman chuckled, grateful to Callender for neatly averting what might have been a tricky situation. The profusion of American medals was a source of constant amusement to RAF aircrew; the story went that USAAF personnel were awarded a medal as soon as they set foot on overseas territory. Well, thought Yeoman, that was their affair, and he could see no reason to get worked up over it. But he knew that some RAF types did get annoyed when they walked into a bar and saw Americans who had yet to undergo their baptism of fire sporting a chestful of medal ribbons.

Yeoman and Callender fell to reminiscing for a while, then followed the general drift towards the dining-room, where the mess staff were desperately trying to cope with the unexpected influx of extra mouths. Lunch consisted of sausages and mashed potatoes, which caused most of the Americans to pull faces and push their plates to one side. Callender smiled.

'I guess they're all a bit mollycoddled,' he said. 'Our rations are first class. After two years of eating steak and ice cream, I don't think I'd be able to get into a Spitfire's cockpit any more.'

Just as they were finishing their lunch, one of the American officers came in and told Callender that the Mustangs were refuelled and ready to go. He nodded and rose from the table.

'Well George, I guess that's it. We'll be on our way.' He grinned. 'If my pilots aren't too pissed to fly, that is.'

Yeoman got up too. 'I'll come down to the field with you,' he said. 'One of my chaps is coming to pick me up in half an hour, anyway, so I might as well have a cup of tea down at 505 Squadron dispersal while I'm waiting. Are you coming too, Tim?'

Phelan shook his head. 'No, I've got a bloody great mound of paperwork about three feet high to get through this afternoon, and the sooner I get started on it the better. So I'll say cheerio to the pair of you, and I'll hope to see you again.' He shook hands with them both, and left.

Yeoman walked to the airfield with Callender, mingling with other American pilots who were heading in the same direction. They stopped by the hangars, for Yeoman wanted to go one way and Callender the other, out to where his Mustang was waiting.

'George,' said Callender suddenly, 'I've been thinking. What are you going to do when all this is over? It can't be long now. Will you stay in the Air Force?'

'I honestly don't know, Jim,' the other replied. 'I stopped thinking about the future a long time ago. As for staying in the Air Force, I don't know about that...I might go back to journalism, try my hand at writing a book, maybe. Did you have any particular reason for asking?'

'Yes, I did. I think that when this war is over, countries all over the world which haven't bothered much about military aviation are going to be in a mad scramble to build up modern air forces. They'll need experienced pilots to train them, like you and me.'

He looked at Yeoman for a moment, then went on: 'I intend to be right there out front, George. Now why don't you give it some thought, too? We were a great team once; we could be again. Just think about it, that's all.'

'Okay, Jim, I will. But a lot can happen in the next few months.'

Callender got the drift of Yeoman's thoughts and laughed.

'Don't worry, George. Remember what you said to me once, when we were being bombed to hell in France? "Only the good die young." So I reckon we don't qualify. We're born survivors, you and I. Be seeing you.'

Yeoman watched him go, knowing that Jim Callender was the best friend he had ever had, hoping fervently that the American's parting remark was a prophetic one.

# Chapter Four

The tiny village of Blackshiels, six miles south of the ancient town of Hawick in the Scottish county of Roxburgh, had once been one of the remotest places in Britain. Its inhabitants had changed little in a thousand years; they had tended their sheep and minded their own business, and when, as sometimes happened, they had been threatened by marauding Scots or English armies, they had simply taken to the hills with their flocks and waited until the fuss had died down before returning to rebuild their ruined homes and picking up the threads of their life again.

World War I had changed everything. Far away in Whitehall, which most of the villagers had never heard of, a nameless general on the War Office staff had picked Blackshiels as a likely site for a new ammunition dump. There were two reasons for this. The first was that a mile to the east of the village there was a large hill, in the eastern slopes of which there were several deep caves connected by natural passages which, with the minimum of engineering problems, could be turned into secure underground bunkers; and the second was that the hill lay some three miles to the west of the railway line that ran southwards from Hawick through Liddesdale to Carlisle, far enough away to make any military transport movements inconspicuous to travellers, but close enough to build a spur line to the hill with comparative ease.

So, for three years, the British Army had become part of the bewildered villagers' existence. Troops had been billeted in the rough houses, had eaten at the family tables, and one or two had married local girls, who were renowned less for their beauty than for their capacity for hard work.

Then, in 1918, had come the Armistice, and the following year the ammunition depot had been closed. The troops had departed, the sheep had returned to the natural shelter of the caves, and only the spur line—soon overgrown with grass—and two or three broken flat cars remained to show that they had ever been. That, and the occasional letter from India or Egypt, written by one of the homesick daughters of the village to her ageing parents.

So, by degrees, things returned to normal, and remained so for a quarter of a century—until one day in April 1944.

A shepherd and his son, searching for errant lambs, toiled slowly up the eastern slopes of the hill that overshadowed the village. Here and there, patches of snow still lay in folds, for winter departed reluctantly from these parts.

The drone of aero-engines came to them suddenly, borne on the wind. The older man did not look up, being intent on his search, but his son scanned the sky carefully.

At first, he saw nothing, although the noise of the engines was growing louder with every second. It was not until he lowered his gaze that he located the aeroplane, and brought a sudden shout from him.

The twin-engined aircraft was racing at high speed along the old spur line, its wing-tips almost touching the embankments on either side, heading straight for the hill. The man and his son stood frozen, unable to take their eyes from it as it rushed headlong towards them, lower than the ridge on which they stood.

At the very last moment it pulled up in a steep climb, passing a few feet over their heads in a thunderclap of sound. Both flung themselves down in the coarse grass as the slipstream buffeted them.

The shepherd struggled to his knees and shook his fist at the aircraft, which was turning steeply, and roared out a string of curses which cast grave doubts on the pilot's parentage. The pilot, however, had not finished yet. Three times more he came thundering up the line, climbing sharply at the end of each run. To the watching men, it seemed almost as if he were trying to fly straight into the mouth of the big cave into which the old line disappeared.

At last, the aircraft gained height and flew away to the south, rapidly dwindling to a speck. The men watched it go, their ears ringing with the crescendo of its engines; then, as silence fell once more over the hillside, they turned back to their search for the lost lamb.

Three days later, the troops returned to the village. There were over a hundred of them, and in a matter of hours the villagers found themselves virtually cut off from the outside world.

A great deal of interest appeared to focus on the hill; all sheep and lambs were rounded up from the area on and around it by the protesting villagers, acting on orders from the military commander, and penned securely a safe distance away, close to the village itself. The villagers continued to protest, both individually and collectively, only to be told curtly that there was a war on and that, for a few days, an air exercise was to be held in the vicinity. The military commander apologized on behalf of the War Office for any inconvenience the villagers might suffer, and they were assured that they would be adequately compensated for any damage to their property or livestock. With that, they had to be content.

Yeoman had chosen the site well. Armed with large-scale maps of England, Scotland and Wales, he had shut himself away in his office for the best part of a day, searching for a combination of tunnel and railway line that closely approximated the tunnels by the River Oise which were used by the enemy as storage depots for their secret weapons.

Three principal enemy tunnels had so far been located, all running into a limestone hill not far from the town of St Leu. Feeding each tunnel, a spur line ran arrow-straight from the main Compiègne—St Quentin line and was about two miles long, flanked in places—although not everywhere—by high embankments. At intervals along the latter, and on the hill itself, the Germans had positioned quadruple 20-mm flak guns.

At the end of the day, a bleary-eyed Yeoman had emerged from his office, triumphantly waving an Ordnance Survey map of the Hawick area, on which he had drawn a large red circle around the village of Blackshiels, its nearby hill and the old disused railway line. On paper it looked first-rate, the contours of the surrounding land matching those of the St Leu area in many respects, and by an extraordinary coincidence the old railway was identical in straightness, length and width between the embankments to those that led to the St Leu tunnels.

All that remained was to work out the details. Yeoman was determined to simulate the actual raid in every respect, and so, for the duration of the intensive training period, he arranged for the squadron to fly north to Wymeswold in Leicestershire—which was then occupied by an Operational Training Unit—because this airfield was almost exactly as far from Blackshiels as St Leu was from Tangmere, the Sussex airfield from which the mission would be flown. The fuel and weapons loads to be carried, and the timing, would be duplicated as exactly as prevailing conditions allowed.

Yeoman and the officer commanding the military detachment, a lieutenant-colonel, went into close consultation over part of the secret target dossier—the part showing only aerial photographs of the objectives, for the lieutenant-colonel was not cleared by Security to know the exact nature of the mission. In the days that followed he and his men reproduced, as faithfully as possible, the positions of enemy flak batteries, setting up dummy guns on the hill overlooking Blackshiels and along the old railway embankment. In this task they were aided by German thoroughness, for the flak guns were sited at equal intervals around each of the three tunnels.

At last, on the morning of 11 April, everything was ready. The sixteen Mosquitos of 380 Squadron took off from Wymeswold and set course northwards, flying straight up the spine of England, the Pennine Hills. A couple of times they ran through a shower of sleet, but it quickly passed and the weather was generally fine, with good visibility.

Each Mosquito carried two dummy 500-lb bombs in its belly. The pilots had been briefed to carry out a first run against the target with bomb-doors closed, to get the lie of the land, and to release their weapons into the mouth of the large cave on the second run. The aircraft were to run-in individually, in line astern. On this first practice mission, the emphasis was on the accuracy of the bomb delivery.

Yeoman, who had carried out a first-hand reconnaissance of the area at low level some days earlier—and, unknown to him, been roundly cursed by the shepherd in the process—led the simulated attack. After all the Mosquitos had made their initial runs, each one came in low along the railway cutting with bomb-doors open, maintaining a steady 250 mph—the best speed for weapon release as the aircraft pulled up steeply at a range of 150 yards, lobbing its bombs in an arc towards the mouth of the cave, or so the experts thought.

After releasing his own bombs, Yeoman climbed to two thousand feet and circled to observe results. He was in radio contact with an observer on the ground, who told him that one of his bombs had hit the target and who continued to call out the scores as the other Mosquitos made their runs.

They were disappointing. Sixty per cent of the practice bombs found the cave mouth, but it was not enough. The

Mosquito crews flew back to Wymeswold for a post-mortem and to prepare for another attempt that afternoon.

It was Rory McManners who came up with a theory to account for their partial failure.

'I think we're too slow,' he said, as the pilots clustered round in one of Wymeswold's briefing-rooms.

'Between the release point and the cave mouth, I think the bombs tend to go unstable in their trajectory and wobble off course—if we release at 250 mph, that is. Why don't we try a shallow dive instead of a long, straight run, say at 300 mph, pull out and release the bombs just as the nose comes up, then climb away up the hillside in a sort of continuous parabola, if you see what I mean? I think the extra fifty miles per hour initial velocity will make all the difference to the bombs' stability, and I'm sure someone can work out the optimum release point.'

Yeoman agreed. 'All right, Rory, we'll give it a try. Attacking on the dive isn't going to be healthy when it comes to the real thing, but if it helps us to place both our bombs accurately, it will be worth it.'

Hardy and a couple of the other navigators put their heads together and made some rapid calculations, coming up after a while with the information that the bombs would have to be released at 220 yards from the tunnel mouth to follow their new trajectory. Terry Saint, who had meanwhile been studying the target photographs—each of which was marked with a scale—also made an interesting observation: on the approach to each of the three tunnels, the Germans had obligingly sited an anti-aircraft battery at a distance of about two hundred yards from the mouth. It would make an excellent aiming-point.

They tried it that afternoon, the Mosquitos arrowing down towards the railway cutting and releasing their bombs to arc across the gap a fraction of a second after pulling out. Then they were away over the hill, the snarl of their engines rattling the roofs and windows of the village beyond.

This time, they had an eighty per cent success rate. And

when they returned the following day the score was even higher, despite the fact that on this occasion the target was partly obscured by smoke drifting from canisters placed near the dummy gun positions in order to simulate what conditions might be like on the real day.

Then the Mosquitos were gone for good, leaving the village to slumber once more, and soon the soldiers had gone too. The only signs left of their presence were a spattering of scars on the hillside and in the cave; mounds of tumbled earth and rock, dislodged by the hurtling projectiles, some of which had buried themselves deep in the soil. None of the villagers would ever know why the tumult had suddenly descended on their lives.

The next day the Mosquitos flew down to Tangmere. Yeoman had sent a signal to Group HQ, stating that the Squadron was ready to undertake the forthcoming operation, and the attack plan had been finalized. The profusion of flak around the objective was a source of worry, and much thought had been given to reducing the danger from it. In the end, it had been decided that each of the three tunnels should be attacked by a section of four Mosquitos to begin with; two of these would dive at the target, as planned, while the other two would stay at low level and shoot up the flak positions on the embankments. These two would then climb away to carry out their own attack on the tunnel, while the original pair would take over the job of flak suppression.

At the same time, a fourth section of four Mosquitos would attack the flak posts on the hill itself with cannon fire before making their bombing runs. Basically, the whole scheme ensured that one pair of Mosquitos would always be available to give covering fire to another. A lot depended on accurate timing, but Yeoman and his pilots were confident that they could pull it off.

If they couldn't do it, they felt, then nobody could.

At Tangmere, the personnel of 380 Squadron, from the CO down to the lowliest airman, had strict instructions to keep themselves to themselves until the operation took place. In the officers' mess, the pilots of the two Spitfire Wings stationed at Tangmere regarded the newcomers with considerable interest, but their attempts at conversation about anything other than trivial matters met with a blank wall of silence and in the end they gave up.

The operation, code-named 'Big Stick', had originally been scheduled to take place in the afternoon of 17 April, but bad weather conditions over the Continent caused it to be postponed for two days. The crews took the opportunity to refresh their memories, for the hundredth time, on the most minute details of the target and the surrounding terrain, poring over maps, target photographs and models, the latter painstakingly built by Flight Lieutenant Freddie Barnes, the Squadron Intelligence Officer, and his small staff. The material was kept in a room under constant guard in the operations block.

At last, in the early hours of 19 April, the weather began to clear and the forecast for the rest of the day was optimistic. At 0600, the main briefing-room was packed with the crews of 380 Squadron and the Spitfire pilots of the Tangmere Wings, who would be covering the Mosquitos during the operation.

After a short address by Tangmere's CO, it was Yeoman who opened the proceedings. Standing on the dais, overlooking the rows of seated men, he began —

'Gentlemen, I know that for the past couple of days there has been a lot of speculation about the presence here of a Mosquito squadron, and that some of you have perhaps resented our silence. The reason for it is quite simply this.

'At 0800, that is in a little under two hours' time, 380 Squadron will carry out a low-level attack against a series of tunnels at St Leu, near the River Oise. These tunnels are being used by the enemy as underground storage depots for a new and devastating type of weapon...'

The audience listened, enthralled and alarmed, as

Yeoman told them the details of the operation. There was much he was not authorized to tell—the specific details of the weapon they were dealing with, for example—but most of the Spitfire pilots now guessed that it was connected in some way with the No-Ball sites which had been under attack for the last three weeks.

After Yeoman had finished, the senior Wing Commander at Tangmere took over the stand, explaining the part to be played by the Spitfires. The three squadrons of 126 Wing would go in fifteen minutes ahead of the Mosquitos and patrol a line between Amiens and Lille in the hope of drawing off enemy fighters, while the squadrons of 127 Wing were to cover the Mosquitos on the way home.

The briefing went on for another half-hour, with various specialist officers adding their own comments. The final act was to synchronize watches, and then the briefing broke up, the aircrew heading for their respective dispersals, where pockets were meticulously emptied of anything which, if anyone was shot down, might give away vital information to the enemy.

In 380 Squadron's dispersal there was little talking; just the odd curt comment, and sometimes a muffled curse as the pilots and navigators struggled into their flying clothing and Mae West lifejackets.

Yeoman looked at his watch: take-off was in twenty minutes. Once again, his mind went over the attack plan.

He would be leading Red Section, which would be attacking the first of the tunnels—'Tunnel Able', as it had been designated. His pilots were Terry Saint, Sergeant Carr and a newcomer to the squadron, Pilot Officer Grinton. 'Tunnel Baker' would be attacked by Yellow Section, consisting of Yves Romilly, Warrant Officer Laurie, Pilot Officer Crombie and Flight Sergeant Martinsen, the latter a Norwegian. Blue Section, led by Rory McManners, with Flight Sergeant Lorrimer, Pilot Officer Wallace and Sergeant Simons would hit 'Tunnel Charlie'.

That left Green Section, under Tim Sloane. He and his

49

pilots—Sergeant Hudson and two more newcomers, Flying Officer Atkins and Flight Sergeant Parker—had the unenviable task of suppressing the flak batteries on the hill before making their own attack after everyone else. It would be up to Sloane—or his deputy, if he was hit—to direct their bombs against whichever of the tunnels appeared to be the least damaged.

It was time to go. Already, the thirty-six Spitfires of 126 Wing were taxi-ing out for take-off. The morning was clear, with a few high mare's tails streaking the sky.

By 0700 all the Mosquitos' engines were turning. A white rocket arced into the sky from the control tower and the sixteen aircraft began to move, section by section, towards the end of the runway.

Yeoman glanced round to ensure that all was well. Terry Saint was in position, to starboard and some distance behind. The other two aircraft of Red Section were astern, keeping well clear to avoid any loose stones that might be whirled up from the runway.

'All set, Happy?'

'All set, skip. Course after take-off is one-two-two, magnetic.'

'Roger.'

The Mosquito began to roll forward, Yeoman eased open the port throttle a little ahead of the other to check the aircraft's slight tendency to swing to port. A light forward pressure on the control column brought the tail up as the Mosquito gathered speed. She bounced once, twice, on the main undercarriage and then she was airborne. Yeoman waited until he had a comfortable margin of height, then braked the wheels—a necessary precaution, for if they were still rotating they would cause severe vibration as they came up into the wells—and raised the undercarriage and flaps.

He turned gently to port, keeping Tangmere in sight, staying low and throttling back a little to enable the others to catch up, carrying out a wide circuit of the airfield. The other Mosquitos came up in pairs and slotted quickly into position. Then, in four tight boxes of four, the whole formation turned on to 122 degrees, drumming out over the coast between the peacetime seaside resorts of Bognor Regis and Littlehampton.

The coast of France lay eighty-five miles ahead of them. Yeoman was aware that their course would take them dangerously close to the anti-aircraft defences around le Tréport, but it could not be helped; a few miles further north they risked running into the Focke-Wulfs from Abbéville, while to the south lay Dieppe—where, since the disastrous landings by the 1st Canadian Division and British Commandos in August 1942 the Germans had stiffened their defences for miles along the coast.

The Mosquitos flew on at a hundred feet. There was no need for Hardy to give the customary warning 'enemy coast ahead'; a few minutes later they could all see it, a hazy blue line rising above the eastern horizon.

A few small boats, fishing-smacks perhaps, blurred past their wing-tips. The Somme Estuary lay over to the left, le Tréport to the right. The eyes of the navigators stared at the terrain ahead, constantly checking that they were on course; those of the pilots roved across the sky, searching ahead, above and to either side.

Both the Mosquitos and the Tangmere Spitfires were using the same radio frequency. So far, the R/T had been silent, but now a crackle of voices, some calm, some excited, burst across it.

'Fantail leader, bandits seven o'clock, level.'

'Roger, keep turning...'

'Here they come!'

'Fantail Yellow Two, break!'

'Red Three, I've had it, baling out.'

Yeoman turned down the volume control until the confused babble of voices was no more than a dull murmur in his headphones. Away to the north, high and invisible, the Spitfires of 126 Wing were engaging the enemy.

'Amiens to port, skipper. Thirty-five miles to target.'

'Roger.' Yeoman glanced over to the left; the town was a blue-grey smudge on the horizon. All the Mosquitos were still in position, as though held together by invisible threads. From time to time, as they sped on, smoky tracer lanced at them from some unseen gun postion, but it was mostly light stuff of machine-gun calibre and their speed quickly took them out of danger.

Soon afterwards, with Montdidier passing close to port, Hardy said quietly:

'Target dead ahead, skipper. Straight down the valley.'

In front of them, less than ten miles away, the ground fell away in a shallow incline towards the valley of the Oise. To the north-west of the river, clearly visible, a hummock of high ground rose in isolation.

Every detail of that hill was implanted on the minds of Yeoman and his fellow pilots. Jutting out from its south-western edge, like shortened fingers, were three spurs—and in the folds of those spurs lay their targets, the tunnels. Some miles beyond the hill, astride the river and the main railway line, lay the towns of Ribecourt and Noyon.

'There are the spur lines,' Hardy said, pointing through the windscreen.

'Okay, I see 'em.' Yeoman pressed the R/T transmit button.

'All Big Stick aircraft, execute attack. Acknowledge.'

One by one, the leaders of the other three sections reported that they had received his order. The formation broke up as each section headed for its respective target.

Terry Saint dropped back until he was half a mile astern of Yeoman's Mosquito, and both climbed to two thousand feet. The other two Mosquitos of Red Section, flown by Carr and Grinton, stayed low, turning along the line of the spur railroad that led to Tunnel Able.

The flak started to come up, spattering the sky ahead with puffs of smoke. Yeoman looked down: Carr and

Grinton had already begun their attack, their Mosquitos racing along the embankments, trailing thin lines of grey smoke as they hammered the flak positions with their cannon.

'All right, Terry, let's go!'

Yeoman pushed the Mosquito's nose down, aiming for the second 20-mm gun emplacement on the approach to the tunnel mouth, the one that would give him the required range of two hundred yards. The Mosquito buffeted slightly, but it was nothing more than the turbulence created by the open bomb doors.

Yeoman tried to close his ears to the shells that were bursting all around with a noise like the deep-throated bark of a dog. Streams of smoke whirled past the perspex of the cockpit canopy.

Somewhere towards the tail of the aircraft there were three distinct thuds, transmitted to him by the vibration of the control column. There was no time to worry about it now. He had eyes only for the gun that was his aiming point, and for the air-speed indicator that would give him the correct speed for bomb release.

The flak gun's four barrels were turned towards him. He could clearly see the flashes from their muzzles. Then the gun disappeared in a cloud of dust and smoke as cannon shells erupted all around it. Out of the corner of his eye he saw Carr's Mosquito streak over the gun emplacement and pull up in a steep climb.

The ASI showed 300 mph. His thumb tensed on the bomb release button, mounted on the control column. In a single movement, he pulled the stick back and jabbed his thumb down.

The Mosquito curved up into a climb. its underside almost brushing the railway line. The two 500-lb bombs fell from its belly, the speed and attitude of the aircraft inserting them into an upward trajectory. They described a beautiful parabola through the air, hit the ground just short of the tunnel mouth with two spurts of dust, and bounced inside.

Yeoman's Mosquito raced up the hillside and over the crest, weaving to escape the flak that reached out to pluck it down. Another Mosquito zipped across its nose, perilously close, its cannon hammering as it engaged one of the flak batteries on the ridge, It was one of Green Section's aircraft, although which one Yeoman could not tell.

Suddenly, a great lump of wing broke away from the Mosquito as it took a direct hit. The remainder went into a fast, uncontrollable roll, shedding fragments, and impacted on top of the battery it had been strafing. There was a blinding flash as its bombs exploded and a great plume of smoke and earth shot into the air.

Sickened, Yeoman did a steep S-turn and took the Mosquito down over the crest of the hill again, flying in the opposite direction to give covering fire to the two Mosquitos which had been strafing the embankment. The latter, having broken away sharply at the end of their strafing runs, were now turning hard, dropping into line astern as they came angling in for their bombing attack.

From the right-hand seat, Hardy glanced back as the tunnel mouth came into view. A huge cloud of evil-looking yellow smoke was billowing from it. Then the navigator winced as the Mosquito's cannon opened up with their usual foot-jarring concussions.

Yeoman fired in short, angry bursts, making as certain as he possibly could that each one was effective, conserving his ammunition. He saw his shells spatter across the armoured shield of an anti-aircraft gun, the explosive impact twisting the barrels like straws.

The Mosquitio lurched suddenly as a shell from the next flak gun in line along the embankment exploded over the port wing with a terrific crack. Yeoman corrected the swing quickly, fired at the gun and missed. Then he was flashing over the top taking the Mosquito up in a fast climb, weaving to escape the glowing trails of fire that chased him.

Terry Saint's Mosquito was also climbing, and Yeoman felt a surge of relief with the knowledge that the irrepressible New Zealander had come through. He called him up over the radio.

'Big Stick Leader to Red Two. Shoot up anything you can see.'

Saint acknowledged and swung round towards the crest of the hill again, firing at some unseen target. Yeoman continued to gain height, bringing the Mosquito round in a wide turn, anxious to find out what was happening. The whole hill was shrouded in smoke; on the crest above Tunnel Able, the wreckage of an aircraft was blazing fiercely.

He looked over towards the other tunnels. Mosquitos twisted and wove across the sky overhead, darting down from time to time to engage troublesome anti-aircraft guns. One of the aircraft flared suddenly with a vivid white flame and went down somewhere beyond the hill. Dark smoke spiralled up in the morning sunlight.

Suddenly, the hill exploded. There was no warning. For three-quarters of a mile along its length, the hill crest gave a sudden heave, as though pushed from underneath by a huge hand. Fissures opened suddenly and spurts of smoke shot through them. Then the hill collapsed on itself, leaving a pall of dust and smoke hanging motionless in the air.

Although he did not know it, Yeoman was witnessing the subterranean explosion of a hundred one-ton warheads, touched off by the Mosquitos' bombs. The warheads had not been stockpiled together, but flame and blast raced through the interconnecting passages below the hill and devastated one store after another. In a large underground hangar, carved out of rock and earth right in the centre of the complex, a thousand tons of débris crashed down on eighty v-i flying-bombs, most of them newly delivered, crushing them into dust. Three hundred German personnel died, many of them mercifully quickly as the hill collapsed on top of them, but others to linger on for days in a nightmare of darkness, hunger, thirst and slow suffocation, hopelessly entombed with no chance of rescue.

Yeoman made a complete circle round the scene of devastation, trying to assess results for the benefit of the Intelligence people. Then he radioed the others.

'All right, chaps, that's it. Good show. Let's go home.'

The Mosquitos turned and set course north-westwards, the sections joining up into formation. One by one, the pilots reported in.

Three aircraft were missing. The Mosquitos flown by Sergeant Carr, of Yeoman's section, and Flying Officer Atkins of Sloane's Green Section were both burning on the hill; it was Atkins' aircraft which Yeoman had seen lose part of its wing as he pulled up from his bomb run, and Carr had apparently failed to pull out in time after making his attack.

And beyond the hill, smoke still boiled upwards from the remains of Rory McManners' Mosquito. No one quite knew what had happened; his number two, Flight Sergeant Lorrimer, had seen the aircraft climb steeply away from attacking a gun emplacement when it had suddenly burst into flames, tipped over and dived almost vertically in the ground. There was no possiblility that the calm, quietly-spoken Scot or his navigator could have survived.

The thirteen surviving Mosquitos flew back the way they had come, bypassing Amiens and keeping the River Somme in sight a few miles off their starboard wing-tips. Poix airfield slid by to the left, but this presented no danger to them; Poix was inhabited by a couple of enemy bomber squadrons, but there were no fighter units there.

The real danger lay to the north of their track, at Abbéville, but the Spitfires of 126 Wing appeared to have done their work well. If the Focke-Wulfs had been air-borne, they would have been drawn off to the north-east, towards Lille, and would now be short of fuel and am-munition. In any event, Yeoman and his crews saw no enemy fighters; but as they crossed the Channel coast the sleek shapes of 127 Wing's Spitfires, sent out to cover their withdrawal, came sliding down from the northern sky and wove protectively overhead, detaching themselves only when the Mosquitos were half-way home.

Yeoman led his Mosquitos into Tangmere at 0915. His first task, on climbing from the cockpit, was to walk round the aircraft and take a look at the damage.

He and Hardy had been lucky. Close to the tail a large patch of fabric had been torn away, and several of the wooden spars were punctured by shell splinters. The port wing, too, was riddled with holes outboard of the engine, and there were jagged rents in the metal of the engine cowling itself. It was a miracle that nothing vital had been hit.

Hardy poked an exploratory finger through one of the holes in the fuselage and grimaced. 'Must do something about these moths,' he said. Then, looking sideways at Yeoman, he added:

'Tough about poor old Rory.'

Yeoman nodded. 'Yes, tough. And the others. Come on, here's the bus.'

The RAF coach deposited the crews outside the de-briefing-room and they tramped inside, slumping wearily at the trestle tables and reaching out to take cigarettes from the packets that had been placed there by one of Freddie Barnes' acolytes. Yeoman and Hardy went over to the table in the centre of the room, the one with the model of the tunnel system on it. The Intelligence Officer was hovering behind it, peering short-sightedly through the lenses of his spectacles at the faces of the aircrews in the room, lines of anxiety furrowing his brow. He waved to a little WAAF aircraft woman, who brought two mugs of tea across for Yeoman and his navigator.

'How did things go?' Barnes asked.

'We lost Rory McManners,' Yeoman replied

wearily. 'Sergeant Carr, too, and Atkins, the new boy. And their navs, of course. No chance of getting out at that height.'

Barnes' face fell. The former schoolmaster would never get used to it, as long as he lived—this snuffing out of young lives, the striking out of names from the nominal roll of a squadron. He blinked rapidly, then, after a pause, he said:

'The target. What about the target?'

Yeoman stretched out an arm and brought his clenched fist down on top of Barnes' model. The papier mache crumpled. 'It blew up,' the pilot said. 'Or rather, it collapsed on top of itself. The whole hill, I mean. We must have touched off something pretty big inside there.'

Barnes sighed, took some more details from Yeoman and Hardy, then went off to confer with the other crews. Thank God, he thought, that it had not all been for nothing. Then, almost immediately afterwards, he felt bitter guilt for allowing the thought to enter his mind; for what cause, however outwardly valid, could justify the brutal extinction of men like McManners? And who would replace them in the years to come?

Had Barnes but known it, Yeoman was thinking along much the same lines. Later, when the bar opened at lunchtime, he ordered six pints of beer, one for each of the men who had not returned. He carried them over to a table in the corner and began to drink them systematically, not speaking to anyone.

The others left him alone, knowing that this was his ritual prelude to the writing of letters to next-of-kin, a job he hated. There had been times in the past, fortunately very few, when Squadron Leader George Yeoman had got very, very drunk.

# Chapter Five

Yeoman and Clive Bowen, whose 373 Squadron had flown into Tangmere a few days earlier, at the beginning of May, sat in deckchairs outside 380 Squadron's dispersal, sheltered from the gusty wind by a small caravan that was used as a rest-room by the armourers. The two men were taking advantage of a period of sunshine, unusually weak for the time of year, that had brightened up what was otherwise a grey and blustery day.

'It doesn't look too promising, George,' Bowen commented, looking up at the clouds that were once more rolling in to extinguish the sun.

His companion agreed. 'I wouldn't like to be those poor bastards out in the Channel,' he said, 'sitting there in the middle of a force five westerly, with damn all to do except be seasick and worry about what they've got coming to them.'

He was referring to the quarter of a million British, American and Canadian troops who, battened below decks in five thousand ships of all shapes and sizes, blind to everthing except the constant misery of nausea, were riding the forbidding waters of the Channel in their various assembly areas. Some of them had been on the vessels for days, praying for the moment when they would be spewed ashore on the coast of France, for shells and bullets would be a merciful alternative to the heaving and tossing of the steel-plated decks and the acrid stench of vomit.

The great armada stretched all the way round the south coast of England, from Cornwall to the Thames, lashed by the spume wind-whipped from the wave crests. Inland, the past few weeks had seen the coastal belt turned into an armed camp, stiff with trucks, guns, armoured fighting vehicles and heavy support equipment. Nothing like it had been known in the history of warfare; and yet, only four years earlier, these same waters had seen the remnants of a defeated army struggling back from the bomb-swept beaches of Dunkirk.

The man whose naval forces had rescued a third of a million men from destruction in 1940 was once again in command of a mighty naval force, one which, if all went well, would enable the Allies to smash a breach in Hitler's 'Atlantic Wall' in just a few more hours. His name was Admiral Sir Bertram Ramsay; it was a name uttered with respect by the men who had once fought in Flanders as boys of eighteen and nineteen. Now, with the campaigns of the Desert and Italy behind them, they were going back to France, supremely confident that this time there would be no retreat.

' "Fair stood the wind for France," ' said Yeoman, quoting vaguely from Drayton's *Battle of Agincourt*.

'What occasioned that sudden burst of poetry?' Bowen grinned. Yeoman smiled back.

'Oh, I don't know, Clive. It's just that...well, I was at Dunkirk, you know, and I can't help feeling a great surge of—pride, I suppose it is. No, that's not it. Pride isn't the right word. Somehow, it's all so—so appropriate. Ourselves...the boys from the Commonwealth...the Yanks... all of us one big force now, bent on giving that little bastard in Berlin just what he deserves after holding most of Europe in slavery for all these years. It's been a long, long haul,' he said, almost to himself.

'When do you think they'll go?' Bowen asked, meaning the invasion fleet.

Yeoman shrugged. 'When the wind drops, I should imagine. Can't keep them sitting out there indefinitely. I hope it's soon, though. I'm getting tired of all this hanging around.'

The squadrons had been on standby for twenty-four hours—as, indeed, had all units of the Allied Expeditionary Air Forces. The aircraft—with the exception of the all-black night fighters—were now sporting broad black-and-white stripes on their wings and fuselages as an aid to identification, for in the confusion that would undoubtedly attend the invasion the anti-aircraft gunners on the ships were certain to open fire on any aircraft that came too close, unless they immediately recognized it as friendly. Also, with large formations of British and American fighters patrolling the beachheads, an operation involving half a dozen different types of aircraft, the possibility of a ghastly mistake was very real.

The aircrews had all been briefed; everyone knew now, after months of total secrecy, that the Allied landings would take place on the coast of Normandy, on a line between the estuaries of the Orne and the Vire.

The task of No. 83 Group's fighters was to provide air cover, by night and day, for the eastern flank of the invasion, where British and Canadian forces would go ashore on three beaches code-named 'Gold', 'Juno' and 'Sword'. Further west, the Americans assaulting 'Utah' and 'Omaha' beaches would be protected by fighters of the USAAF.

Clive Bowen's Mosquito night fighters were likely to be the first in action, for—together with other Mosquito night fighter units—they were to patrol the enemy coastline from Cap Gris Nez to Cherbourg, on the lookout for German aircraft attempting to attack the invasion fleet as it moved across the Channel under cover of darkness. From dawn onwards, while single-engined day fighters provided an umbrella over the beaches, the Mosquito fighter-bomber squadrons of the 2nd Tactical Air Force—of which Yeoman's No. 380 was now part— would fly 'Ranger' sorties deep into enemy territory beyond the beach-heads, shooting up enemy airfields and communications. For this task, the aircraft would usually operate in pairs.

There was nothing to do now but wait. Later, when Bowen went off to join his crews at their final briefing for the night's operations, Yeoman wandered disconsolately round the airfield, itching to get into the air, but knowing that his squadron would not be allowed to cross the Channel until the invasion had actually begun. This restriction was placed on all aircrew who had knowledge of where the landings would take place, for obvious reasons of security.

Yeoman wondered where Julia was tonight, and whether she had a newspaper assignment connected with the coming invasion in some way. Luckily for his peace of mind, he was unaware of her involvement with the Special Operations Executive. They had not met for some time now, but by letter and telephone they had arranged to spend a weekend in London as soon as it was mutually convenient. It seemed to Yeoman, that their times off duty were doomed never to coincide.

He wished that she were with him now, to share this momentous piece of history. It seemed an age since those days they had shared together in France, fleeing one step ahead of the German panzers; days when she had told him, with the utmost conviction, that America would one day be fighting alongside Britain in this war.

He had not quite believed her, then, but her prediction had turned out to be true. Nevertheless, despite all the aid they had given, despite all the lend-lease, he doubted very much whether the Americans would ever have entered the war had it not been for the attack on Pearl Harbour by Japan, Germany's Axis partner. But perhaps, he told himself, that was uncharitable. In a sense this had been America's war right from the start, thanks to adventurers and idealists, men like his friend Jim Callender, who had made it their fight long before that day of infamy in December 1941.

Immediately after dinner Yeoman made a tour of the Mess, to round up anyone he could find from his squadron and tell them to go to bed; they were likely to be up well before dawn. He need not have bothered. The anteroom and the bar were empty; it seemed that everyone had made an individual decision that tomorrow might be a rough day and had turned in early. Yeoman smoked a last pipe and followed their example.

It must have been one o'clock in the morning, that earthshaking morning of 6 June 1944, which would forever be known as D-Day, when Yeoman awoke from a fitful sleep. He shook his head to clear it and got out of bed, crossing to the window and opening it wide.

A rising moon, little more than a quarter full, spread its glow over the coast and the Channel beyond. Although he could not see the latter, which was some four miles distant beyond Bognor Regis, he could visualize the great mass of ships which must now be heading in a solid phalanx for their objective on the shore of Occupied France.

The sky was filled with the sound of hundreds of aero-engines. The night vibrated and shuddered with them; the continual roar battered the ears and numbed the senses.

They came in wave after wave, those invisible aircraft, skimming through the moonlit shreds of wind-driven cloud, laden with paratroops or towing gliders; the spearhead of the invasion. Yeoman did not envy the glider pilots, who would have to grope their way down through the night to a precarious landing in the fields of Normandy, with their natural obstacles of high hedgerows. It needed a particular kind of courage to do that sort of job.

Yeoman closed the window and went back to bed, but the roaring overhead continued almost unabated and sleep proved impossible. By the time his batman tapped on the door at 0300, bearing the inevitable cup of dark brown and lukewarm tea (which Yeoman invariably tipped down the washbasin as soon as the man had left, so as not to hurt his feelings) the pilot was up, shaven and dressed.

Dawn was breaking as he ate breakfast, in company with several other drowsy pilots and navigators of his squadron. Outside, across the airfield, there was a sudden roar of massed Merlin engines: the Spitfire boys were already taking off for the beaches.

Yeoman himself took off on 380 Squadron's first D-Day patrol an hour later, with Warrant Officer Laurie as his number two. The idea was for the Squadron's Mosquitos to operate in pairs throughout the morning, taking off at thirty-minute intervals, penetrating French territory east of the invasion area and circling round to attack targets of opportunity immediately to the rear of it.

As he climbed out over the Channel, Yeoman was pleasantly surprised to find that the weather conditions were better than he had expected; the forecast had been bad for several days past, but now he found that the cloud base was more than two thousand feet and visibility at least six miles.

Below the speeding Mosquito, the Channel was an awe-inspiring sight. As far as the eye could see, stretching away to starboard, the arrowhead wakes of ships made white furrows in the slate grey of the sea. Above the armada a forest of barrage balloons drifted, silvery blobs against the clouds.

As the Mosquitos approached the French coastline near Honfleur, with Le Havre off their port wing-tips, the eastern sector of the Allied beachhead slid into view. Some distance offshore, two great battleships, standing broadside on to the beach, were hurling salvoes of shells at some target inland, the smoke of their 15-in guns boiling out across the water. More smoke, shot with twinkling flashes, obscured the landing areas.

The Mosquitos pushed inland towards Lisieux, following a parallel road and railway-line that cleaved their way through a valley winding between wooded hillsides. Just short of the town they came upon a train, steaming its way towards the coast, and shot it up with their cannon, leaving it stopped with the locomotive spurting satisfactory clouds of smoke; then, skirting the town to avoid the flak concentrations there, they swung in a broad turn to starboard, following the railroad as it veered off towards Caen.

Five miles west of Lisieux, the line passed through a long tunnel. It had been heavily bombed and blocked by the 2nd Tactical Air Force on numerous occasions, but the enemy had an unlimited supply of forced labour and it had been unblocked just as quickly. Yeoman knew that it had been attacked again the previous evening, during the massive air strikes that had been a prelude to the invasion, but he had decided to take a look at it none the less, and had ordered each Mosquito to be armed with two 500-lb bombs.

The ground around the railway-line looked like the surface of the moon, pock-marked for miles with a rash of craters. The line, however, appeared to be intact, and as they swept on Hardy spotted a plume of steam, rising into the morning air.

It was a train all right, a big locomotive pulling a line of flat cars which appeared to be laden with tanks, and as they drew nearer the first part of it vanished into the tunnel like a snake slithering into its underground burrow.

Yeoman called up Laurie on the R/T. There were only seconds in which to act.

'Get this end of the tunnel,' he yelled. 'I'm going for the other end!'

He pulled back the stick, leap-frogging over the high ground just as the train's tail disappeared into the darkness. He swept over the ridge and brought the fighter-bomber curving round towards the other end of the tunnel, about a mile distant on the other side of the hill, lowering the bomb-doors as he did so. He would use the same technique as the Mosquitos had employed against the V-I tunnels at St Leu, diving at a shallow angle and then tossing the bombs at the tunnel mouth.

The round, dark maw of the tunnel yawned at him through the perspex of the windscreen. He dropped the nose a little, aiming a couple of hundred yards short, and watched his speed build up to 300 mph. Then he pulled back on the stick, pressed the bomb release, heard the 'clunk' of the missiles falling away, held the Mosquito in a steady ten-degree climb for a moment to ensure that they dropped cleanly from the weapons bay, then hauled back hard so that the Mosquito bounced towards the clouds as though tossed from a catapult.

Yeoman kept up the pressure on the stick, pulling the aircraft into the beginning of a loop, then half-rolled out into level flight, looking back as he did so.

Where the tunnel mouth had been there was a tumbled mass of earth and rock. The railway tracks leading to it were buckled and twisted at grotesque angles. Yellow smoke drifted away on the breeze and clouds of chalky dust settled slowly on the hillside.

Laurie's Mosquito slid into view and came alongside, rocking its wings. Yeoman pressed the R/T button:

'Did you hit it okay, Arthur?'

'Right on the nose, Boss.' There was no trace of excitement in the Canadian's drawl. 'Just like a cork in a bottle. It'll take 'em a while to dig that bastard out.'

Yeoman smiled. 'All right, we'll go south-west for a while, towards Falaise. Keep your eyes skinned: the Luftwaffe is bound to be around somewhere.'

But the Lufwaffe was absent from the sky. The two Mosquitos roved back and forth over the area south of Caen for the best part of an hour, and never saw a single German aircraft. In the end, keeping well clear of the battle area of the Normandy beaches, they turned north-west and flew at low level up the Cherbourg Peninsula, using up their remaining ammunition in a series of devastating passes against an enemy convoy which they found moving slowly south along a congested road from Valognes. With the smoke of burning vehicles staining the sky behind them, jinking furiously to escape the glowing streams of flak that reached out vengefully towards them, they opened their throttles and slipped over the coast, unscathed except for a few small holes which Laurie had collected in his rear fuselage.

The sixteen Mosquitos of 380 Squadron went out time and again in the course of the day, some of the crews flying three sorties, and all returned with the same story: they had found plenty of ground targets, but never a sign of the Luftwaffe. Yeoman knew that the Luftwaffe squadrons in the Normandy area were far from strong, with only about three hundred fighters, bombers and fighter-bombers between them, but even so it was strange that they had not put in an appearance. His guess was that, severely outnumbered, they had pulled back to airfields in the rear as soon as the invasion had started to avoid the danger of being wiped out on the ground, but in all probability they would soon be hurled into the fray, reinforced by other units drawn from the defence of Germany.

The Spitfire boys, in particular, were practically foaming at the mouth with frustration. They had been anticipating this day for weeks, confident in their skills and prowess, eager for a chance to come to grips with the enemy as never before—and nothing had happened. Instead, they had flown their interminable patrols up and down the beaches, been shot at by the guns of their own ships—despite the striped markings on their aircraft and the 'foolproof' recognition signals—and, forced to remain at less than two thousand feet because of the cloud base, had risked being blown out of the sky by the heavy salvoes of the warships, whose huge shells the pilots could sometimes clearly see as they screamed inland to pulverize some distant objective.

The only truly comforting fact at the end of the day was that the Allied invasion force had succeeded in establishing a foot-hold on the continent of Europe, and it was the overwhelming weight of Allied air power which had enabled it to do so. In more than eleven thousand sorties flown by the Allied Air Forces on 6 June, not one single aircraft had been lost to the Luftwaffe.

The Luftwaffe came after dark, and the night-fighting Mosquitos of Clive Bowen's 373 Squadron were there to meet them. At 0030 on 7 June, one Mosquito navigator after another picked up radar contacts, heading for the fires on and around the beaches, and steered the pilots towards them.

Fourteen Dornier 217 bombers of a special duties unit known as Kampfgruppe 100—the same unit which, on a terrible night in November 1940, had led the devastating attack on the British city of Coventry—tried to break through the night fighter screen to attack the warships and supply vessels that lay offshore.

Under its wings, each bomber carried two Henschel 293 glider bombs, known to the Luftwaffe crews by the code-name of 'Fritz-X'. After launch, they were designed to be steered to the target by radio signals, the bomb-aimer keeping track of the missile in the darkness by means of a red flare in its tail.

Two of the bombers got through and released their Fritz-Xs, one of which struck a freighter at the waterline and blew a hole in her. Two more Do 217s were shot down by the murderous flak, and seven fell to the guns of 373 Squadron and other Mosquito units operating in the area.

Clive Bowen himself shot down one of them, and his subsequent combat report told the story in laconic terms.

PILOTS PERSONAL COMBAT REPORT
373 SQUADRON

83 Group/Tangmere
Date: 6/7 June 1944
A/c No. and Type: 373/P Mosquito XII 779
Captain: S/L Bowen
Navigator: F/L Wells

Planned Serrate Patrol: Patrol 'F' Elbeuf—Breteuil—Argentan—Vire—Caen.
Planned Serrate Route: Base—Cap de la Hève—Patrol—Pointe de Barfleur—Base.

When 5 miles SE of Caen at 0045 hrs at 9,000 ft, a Serrate contact was obtained dead ahead. We followed on our approximate course, losing height for 14 mins at 260 IAS. Radar contact was then obtained left and below and agreed with Serrate (maximum range). Mosquito continued to lose height to 5,000 ft, and at this height visual was obtained at 1,500 ft range. Great difficulty was experienced in identifying enemy aircraft on account of dark night and also as enemy aircraft was now climbing. We followed on A1 with occasional switch to Serrate, and after further visual the enemy aircraft's identity was finally established as a Dornier 217. All this time the enemy aircraft was taking no evasive action.

Fire was opened at 200 ft and strikes were seen between fuselage and starboard engine, which burst into flames. Enemy aircraft turned port and then went down in a spiral dive to starboard, burning all the time. Mosquito followed enemy aircraft as it fell and saw an explosion on the ground as it hit.
Position: 49 14N 00 55w at 0110 at 8,000ft.
Rounds Fired: 80 x 20-mm. No stoppages.
Camera Exposed.

NB Navigator had several other Serrate contacts at the same time as initial one and selected the strongest. All the others were right on top of scale (about 510 m/cs.) Enemy aircraft appeared to carry some form of large bombs or fuel tanks under wings, jettisoned as soon as we opened fire.

Signed: C. F. Bowen
Captain of Aircraft


The combination of airborne interception radar and 'Serrate', the device that enabled the Mosquitos to home on to radar transmissions from enemy aircraft, had long since proved to be deadly, and the crews of 373 Squadron were understandably jubilant over this big success on the first night of the invasion. The other Tangmere squadrons added their congratulations, but it was galling for them to have flown so many patrols and to have seen nothing.

The Luftwaffe, it seemed, was being very cautious, carefully husbanding its reserves of combat aircraft by sending them against the beachheads only under cover of darkness. In view of the swarms of Allied fighters patrolling the coast, it was an understandable precaution.

Nevertheless, a few enemy aircraft did venture into the invasion area by day; not many of them survived. Shortly before noon on 7 June, for example, a wing of Spitfires from Manston pounced on a dozen Junkers 88s which dropped out of the clouds over Arromanches and promptly shot half of them down in flames; the remainder hastily jettisoned their bombs and escaped into the overcast again.

Fittingly, it was Yves Romilly who scored 380 Squadron's first victory after D-Day. It happened as the sun was setting on 7 June.

Romilly was patrolling the area to the south of Caen, watching the bloated blood-red sun sinking through the smoke of the battle area and thinking of turning for home after what had so far been a fruitless sortie, when his navigator gave a sudden excited shout over the intercom.

'There's an aircraft at two o'clock, low! No, *two* aircraft, I think...I can't make it out.' The man's voice was bewildered.

Romilly dropped the Mosquito's starboard wing, and saw why, Cruising along at about two thousand feet, heading in the general direction of the American sector of the invasion front, was the weirdest contraption he had ever seen in the air.

He could readily appreciate his navigator's confusion, for at first sight it looked like two aircraft flying in an impossibly close formation, one on top of the other. Then the thing went into a turn, and he saw that the two aircraft—the top one now identified as a Focke-Wulf 190 and the one underneath as a Junkers 88—were in fact joined together.

'Good Lord,' the navigator said in astonishment. '*Now* what are the bastards up to?'

'Let's go down and find out,' muttered Romilly, and pushed forward the stick, taking the Mosquito in a long dive towards the target.

The Fw 190/Ju 88 combination cruised on serenely; there was no indication that the Mosquito had been sighted. Romilly closed in steadily to a hundred yards, his thumb caressing the firing button.

At that moment, the two aircraft in his sights abruptly parted company. The Junkers 88 flew straight on, while the Focke-Wulf began a sharp climbing turn to port. Romilly raised the nose a little, put on some left rudder and gave the 190 a two-second burst with his cannon.

The result was spectacular. His shells struck the Focke-Wulf's wing root and a fraction of a second later the whole wing tore away. The remainder of the 190 flicked into a series of incredibly fast rolls and twisted earthwards, dragging a plume of smoke. It slammed into the ground a few moments later, narrowly missing some farm buildings.

Without waiting to observe the Focke-Wulf's fate Romilly hauled the Mosquito round and went after the Ju 88, which was flying straight and level half a mile away. He missed with his first burst, misjudged his speed badly and overshot the target, swearing fluently in a mixture of French and English.

As he turned to make a second attack, his navigator said quietly, in a voice that registered disbelief:

'Yves, there's nobody in the 88's cockpit.'

Romilly, stifling his urge to shoot the Junkers out of the sky immediately, decided to take a close look at the enemy aircraft; there might be something of interest here for the Intelligence people.

His navigator was right. Formating right alongside the Junkers, he looked across into the 'glasshouse' cockpit. There was no one at the controls, or at the rear gun position. In fact, there was no rear gun at all, although just aft of where it ought to have been there were some funny-looking radio aerials.

He shot some film at close range, to give the experts back home something to work on. Then, since they were now dangerously close to the invasion area, he dropped back a little and opened fire on the Junkers. His shells blew off part of the 88's tail and the aircraft swung into a ponderous spiral dive. After a quick glance round to make sure that the sky above and behind was empty he followed it down and saw it impact on the edge of a field.

A huge explosion rippled across the ground. The shock wave hit the Mosquito a second later, tossing it up like a leaf and almost turning it over on its back. A badly shaken Romilly managed to regain control and found to his relief that everything still seemed to be working all right. Putting the aircraft into a climbing turn, he looked down: in the field where the Junkers had crashed there was a massive crater, surrounded by a great spread of scattered earth. A mushroom of smoke hung over it.

'It must have been packed to the gunwales with explosive,' said Romilly's navigator, wiping the sweat from his forehead as they headed out to sea. 'Radio-controlled, probably. Very ingenious.'

Ingenious it certainly was, and the Fw 190/Ju 88 combination might have proved deadly too, had the enemy used it in sufficient numbers against the Allied invasion fleet. The German name for it was 'Mistel'—Mistletoe—and, as Yves Romilly and his navigator had discovered, it involved a Junkers 88 whose fuselage had been converted into a big 4,000-lb hollow-charge bomb, guided to its target by a Fw 190 mounted on its back. During the flight, the engines of the Ju 88 provided the motive power; the pilot of the Focke-Wulf switched on his engine just before release, dropped the

Junkers, which he steered to its target by radio, and then did a smart about-turn back to base.

As it was, the few Mistels that did attempt to approach the invasion area were soon shot out of the sky, the lumbering combinations proving easy prey for the Allied fighters. Nevertheless, their use indicated that the Luftwaffe still had a few tricks up its sleeve, and the Allied pilots could not help wondering what alien weapons they would encounter next.

They were not kept guessing for long.

# Chapter Six

Yeoman and Julia Connors strolled arm-in-arm down the long, straight slope of Constitution Hill, past the high wall that surrounded Buckingham Palace Gardens, surmounted by blackened strands of savage-looking barbed wire.

They were allowing themselves the luxury of going nowhere in particular. It was a sunny Sunday morning, and after a short ride on the underground from Earls Court, where Julia shared an apartment with two other girls (both of whom had fortunately been absent for the past few days) they had emerged at Hyde Park Corner and wandered off in the general direction of the Victoria Embankment.

Julia looked sideways at Yeoman and gave his arm a little squeeze.

'You still don't look well, love,' she said, with mild concern in her voice.

Yeoman smiled. 'It's nothing more than good, healthy exhaustion,' he joked. 'After all, you haven't been letting me get much sleep...Seriously, I feel fine. Stop fussing, woman, or I shall smack your pretty bottom. Again.' He turned a wolfish grin on her and she fell silent, happily drinking in the sights and sounds around them, humming a little nondescript tune to herself.

Inwardly, Yeoman felt far from well, although considerably better than he had done five days earlier when the Station Medical Officer at Tangmere, after subjecting him to a thorough examination, had immediately sent him packing on a week's leave.

Yeoman had not realized, until that moment, how much his physical health had deteriorated. He was a stone below his normal weight, he suffered from frequent eyestrain and dizzy spells, and he found it increasingly difficult to make speedy, balanced decisions.

Squadron Leader George Yeoman, in short, was suffering from the cumulative effects of four years of operational flying—air combat duty, as the Americans would call it—with only relatively short rests in between. He was almost completely worn out.

The SMO had fortunately recognized the symptoms in time. He knew of too many pilots who had become the victims of their own frayed nerves and battered reflexes. The first sign of impending disaster was when they started to 'push their luck'—making two or three strafing runs over an enemy airfield, for example, when everyone else made only one. After that, disintegration was often rapid, with reactions slowing down to the point where they were no longer adequate even for the task of flying a high-performance aircraft, let alone engaging in combat. So Yeoman, protesting, had been bundled off to London for the rest; but his protests had ceased when he had learned that Julia, too, could manage a few days off duty.

Despite Julia's closeness, however, Yeoman had found his mind turning again and again to thoughts of the Squadron, and he had to fight hard to resist frequent impulses to ring Tim Sloane, his deputy, to find out how things were going. Such an act, he knew, would not be fair to Sloane, for it would imply a lack of trust in the efficiency of the flight lieutenant, and with Sloane in line for a squadron of his own he wished to do nothing that might undermine the man's confidence.

Nevertheless, he was sorry that his enforced leave had come at a time when the tempo of air operations was at a peak, when the Allies were consolidating their foothold in Normandy and preparing to break out of the bridgehead.

Then, with the Allied Air Forces stretched to the utmost in support of operations on the ground, a new and terrible menace had reared its head to tax their resources and skill even further.

Yeoman had left Tangmere for London in the evening of Monday, 12 June. A few hours later, the Germans had fired the first salvoes of what they called 'Operation Rumpelkammer', launching four v-1 flying-bombs across the Channel. The first of them had exploded at Swanscombe, in Kent, at exactly 0418 hours on the thirteenth.

Four bombs hardly constituted the massed assault envisaged by Hitler; the attentions of the Allied Air Forces had destroyed all chances of that. Nevertheless, the threat posed by these deadly, impersonal projectiles was serious enough, and—coming as it did at this stage in the war, just as victory was beginning to creep into sight—it had a vicious effect on the morale of Londoners who had already weathered the agony of one Blitz. Moreover, the v-1s came as a complete surprise to the civilian population; although the government had been expecting the attack to start for some time, it had remained a well-kept secret.

The v-1s, trailing red flame from their tails, their engines making a noise like a two-stroke motor cycle, had been plunging to earth in and around London at intervals throughout the week; almost everyone in the city and on the approaches to it had seen and heard them, and with characteristic humour had nicknamed them 'Doodlebugs'. Nevertheless, it was not until 16 June that the Minister of Home Security, Herbert Morrison, had officially told the public what was happening.

Yeoman had read it in the *Daily Mail* on Saturday morning, and had allowed himself a sardonic smile. Among other things, the Minister had said: 'The enemy's aim is clearly, in view of the difficulty of his military situation, to try to upset our morale and interfere with our work. It is essential that there should be the least possible interruption in all work vital to the country's needs at this time, and the Government's counsel is that everyone should get on with his or her job in the ordinary way and take cover only when danger is imminent.'

Fine, thought Yeoman. Except that the interval between a v-1's motor cutting out and the missile hitting the ground was about fifteen seconds, which didn't leave a lot of time for diving into the nearest shelter.

They walked around the north side of Memorial Gardens, crossed the Mall and entered St James's Park. They encountered a few strollers, some in uniform and some not, but not as many as Yeoman had expected; then, glancing at his watch, he realized that the more devout—and their numbers had grown substantially over the past few years, as though religion had become a kind of insurance policy against the worst that war could throw at them—would be at church.

'Let's sit down,' Julia said suddenly, pulling Yeoman towards a park bench. 'We don't know how long the sunshine is going to last. We may as well soak it up while we can.'

They sat for a long time, in the dappled sunlight. Julia plucked a sprig of yellow laburnum blossom and fastened it to her lapel of her light green uniform, on which shoulder flashes proclaimed her trade of war correspondent. Only a handful of people knew that Julia Connors followed another trade, one infinitely more dangerous and taxing, and only she could appreciate how much these moments of peace and tranquillity meant to her, far from the darkness of Occupied Europe and the nerve-racking, sickening fear that gripped her when, roused by some noise in the night, she lay soaked in her own sweat, clutching the gun that was her constant bedside companion, waiting for the pounding on the door....

'Are you all right?'

Yeoman was looking at her, a puzzled expression on his face. With a shock, she realized that she was trembling, her heart pounding furiously, perspiration standing out on her face. She pulled herself together with a supreme effort.

'Sorry, darling.' She managed a weak smile. 'Yes, I'm okay. Just felt a little chilly breeze for a moment, that's all. It brought me out in goose-pimples. I'm all right, really. Now who's fussing?'

Yeoman smiled, but the morning was still and warm, with no trace of a breeze, and he sensed that something was amiss. He knew better, though, than to press the point; she would tell him in her own good time, if she so wished.

He had noticed the change in her as soon as they had met again. Beautiful and loving she still was; but her infectious humour bubbled to the surface far less frequently than it had done in the past, and the tension in her was apparent. There were lines and shadows around her eyes, and her sleep, once deep and untroubled in his arms, was now fitful and disturbed, as though her subconscious mind was haunted by some awful spectre.

It hurt him to see her like this, left him with a feeling of helplessness. He could cope with most things, but not this. Sometimes, over the past week, he had looked at her and felt a deep and unaccountable sense of foreboding, as though the pair of them were standing on the edge of a chasm that would soon gape wide to swallow up one or both of them for ever.

From Julia's point of view, the worst thing of all was that she was aware of his feelings, and yet in her turn there was nothing she could do to reassure him. She longed to hold him, to tell him everything, that the nightmare in which she was ensnared would soon be over, that they could both awaken to the daylight and the sun; but she knew she never could, not for a long, long time to come.

So instead she sat there with him, on the bench in St James's Park, and made meaningless small-talk about the price of vegetables—carrots four shillings and sixpence per bunch, no less, and peas and beans three shillings a pound—about the books they had read in recent months and the film they had seen the other evening. They had had a friendly argument about that; Yeoman had wanted to go the the Plaza in Piccadilly Circus to see *Lady in the Dark* ('The Most-Discussed Picture of the Year—Radiant Revelations of a Woman's Secret Desires', or so the posters had proclaimed) while Julia's choice had been *The Eve of St Mark* at the Odeon in Leicester Square ('Sensational Long-Run Play Becomes a Love Story so Poignant that Millions will Make it Their Own!')

In the end they had stood in the middle of the road and spun a coin, which had fallen down a drain, and so, laughing, they had gone to the Carlton instead to see Gary Cooper and Ingrid Bergman in Hemingway's *For Whom the Bell Tolls*, and both agreed afterwards that it had been a wise choice.

An old lady, wearing a threadbare black coat and a shiny hat of matching colour with a bunch of artificial cherries dangling from it over one ear, waddled up to their bench and flopped down on it, settling herself with a long sigh. Then, peering at them with a rheumy gaze, she asked:

'Mind if I join you, dearies? Lovely morning, isn't it?'

Julia smiled, agreeing that it was, and that they didn't mind in the least.

The old woman squinted at Yeoman's uniform and embarked on a long, rambling monologue as she unwrapped some sandwiches from a grubby piece of greaseproof paper.

'Air Force, eh? Wish you'd do something about them things.' She rolled her eyes skywards, and Yeoman assumed that she was referring to the v-is.

'Can't get any sleep nowadays,' she grumbled. 'Worse than during the Blitz. At least you knew when the Jerries were coming over, then. There's no warning with these bloody things. All times of the day and night. The Jones family had their roof blown off last night, and now my cat's missing. Probably gone to ground somewhere. Can't say as I blame the poor little bugger, must be scared out of his wits.'

She broke off a piece of crust and hurled it at a sparrow, which side-stepped adroitly and then seized the morsel in its beak, carrying it off into the bushes.

'Do you live nearby?' asked Julia, conversationally. The old woman glared at her, then emitted a shrill cackle.

'Yes, ducks, 'course I do. That's my house, over there.' She gestured towards Buckingham Palace. Then, as though regretting her sarcasm, she said: 'No, lovey, not me. Born and bred in Stepney, I was; top end of Whitehorse Road. Not much left out that way, now,' she went on mournfully. 'Caught a packet during the Blitz, we did. And now these bloody things.' She rolled her eyes expressively heavenwards again.

She rubbed her right eye, brushing away a real or imagined tear. 'Live all on me own now, I do,' she said. 'Have done since when my Tom was took with the influenza. Went all through the last war without a scratch, too, he did, then along comes the bloody influenza and takes him off.'

She crammed the last of her sandwiches into her mouth and chewed it furiously.

'Only pleasure I get, these days,' she said through a mouthful of crumbs, 'coming out here with my sandwiches when it's sunny and strolling round the parks. Well, I'll be off.'

She rose on creaking limbs and walked away around the end of the lake in the direction of Birdcage Walk, a stooped huddle of black gradually diminishing amid the summer greenery and blossoms.

They watched her go in silence, neither speaking for some moments, Yeoman took out his pipe and tamped tobacco into the bowl.

'Poor old thing,' Julia said suddenly. 'All alone like that, with no one to care for her.'

Yeoman gave an unsympathetic grunt. 'You shouldn't take people at face value,' he admonished, half in jest. 'She was probably waiting for one of us to give her a few shillings so that she could go and drown her sorrows. She reminded me of an old woman who used to tramp the roads around North Yorkshire when I was a boy, begging from house to house; she collapsed and died by the roadside one day, and they found a fortune in five-pound notes stitched into the lining of her coat.'

Julia looked at him, aghast.

'George Yeoman!' she exclaimed. 'What a horribly cynical thing to say! The poor woman probably hasn't had a square meal in months. Why, I've half a mind to go after her and—

The strident howl of an air-raid siren distant and spine-chilling, cut through her sentence, Its harsh notes were taken up by another, much closer.

Julia's eyes were wide and frightened, and Yeoman thought: my God, she can't take it any more. She's burnt out inside.

She stepped close to him and gripped his arm. 'Should we find a shelter?' she asked tremulously. He placed a comforting arm round her shoulders and brought her closer still.

'No, let's stay here. Out in the open, and the sun. It might be a false alarm, anyway.'

But it was real enough. A few moments later, they both heard the strange uncanny mutter in the sky that heralded the approach of a flying-bomb. The noise grew steadily louder, and now there was no longer any doubt that the bomb was heading in their direction.

Yeoman looked round and spotted a huge, gnarled oak tree fifty yards away. Taking Julia by the hand, he trotted over to it and they stood together in the shelter of its trunk, pressing themselves apprehensively against it as the noise increased in volume until it blotted out all other sounds.

Julia clasped both hands to her ears, closing her eyes. Yeoman moved until her body was between his own and the tree trunk, holding her close to him.

'For God's sake don't stop,' Julia whispered, praying

to the soulless mechanical device that was bearing down on them, as yet unseen. 'For God's sake keep going.'

The motor stopped. In the sudden silence, a bird sang.

Julia was trembling violently, her fists clenched now. Yeoman held her tighter, unconscious of the fact that he was holding his breath.

There was an eternity of waiting in which time froze.

The explosion, when it came, was surprisingly dull, but the blast and shock-wave that accompanied it were violent enough. The earth heaved under them, throwing them temporarily off balance, and the blast wave that ripped across the park tore branches brutally from the trees.

The stout oak sheltered Yeoman and Julia from the effects of the blast, but twigs and leaves showered down on them. A little bird struck the tree trunk and fluttered to the ground dying, its neck broken.

Yeoman stepped from the shadow of the oak and looked out across the park. On the far side, beyond the narrow lake, a great pall of dust and smoke rose into the sky where the park joined Birdcage Walk.

'Come on!' Yeoman seized Julia's hand and they ran across the little bridge that joined the two halves of the park, heading for the mushrooming smoke. In the distance they could hear the bells of ambulances and fire engines. A few people were standing motionless, staring fixedly at the smoke as though dazed; others were converging on the scene of the disaster. The sharp odour of sap, released when the blast tore bark from the trees hung over everything.

They reached the edge of Birdcage Walk and stopped dead in their tracks, horrified and stunned by the scene of devastion that met their eyes. 'Oh, sweet Jesus,' Julia said softly, 'it's hit the Guards Chapel.'

Where the chapel had stood, on the edge of Wellington Barracks, there was now only a great mound of rubble, shrouded in smoke, grit and dust.

Rescuers, many of them Guardsmen, were already at

work, tearing at the débris with their bare hands or any tools they could find.

The Guards Chapel, in its picturesque setting close to the Palace, had always been a favourite place of worship. On this bright Sunday morning of 18 June 1944, it had been packed. The final tally of the tragedy, after many hours of toil among the wreckage, would be 121 dead and 68 seriously injured, the majority of them Servicemen and women.

Yeoman would never have a clear memory of the next few hours—hours filled with murderous thirst, choking dust and sweat as he and Julia toiled alongside the other rescuers.

The task was nightmarishly difficult. The walls still stood, forming an enclosure that was choked with bricks, mortar and massed chunks of grey concrete; every entrance was blocked solid, and it was not until someone discovered a way in behind the altar that the rescuers were able to reach the dead and the injured, whose pitiful, dust-smothered cries made the morning hideous.

Julia had been an auxiliary nurse during the London Blitz of 1940 and had become hardened to the sight of death and mutilation, yet she wept as the crushed and broken bodies were brought from the rubble, the tears making long furrows down her dust-grimed face. The children were the worst... two little girls in their pretty summer frocks, lying silent and still beside their parents, a Grenadier Guards officer and his wife, a whole family wiped out brutally in an instant of time.

The horror went on for hour after hour. Yeoman, his once-spotless uniform now caked with filth, his hands bloody and raw, worked shoulder to shoulder with two young soldiers, their faces white with shock, burrowing into a black tunnel to free two ATS girls. One of the latter, her face a mask of blood, clutched the pilot's sleeve and whispered hoarsely:

'Please, please, get me out into the light. I can't move my legs. Don't let me die down here. I want to see the sun.'

'You aren't going to die,' Yeoman reassured her. 'We'll get you out. And don't worry about your legs; it's just temporary shock, that's all.'

They got her into the fresh air and laid her on a stretcher. She moved her head, looking up at the sky and over towards the park, where the birds still sang; then she gave a tiny smile, and died.

Members of the Salvation Army, the Women's Voluntary Service and the Red Cross moved among the rescuers and the rescued like ministering angels, distributing mugs of tea which was like nectar to parched, dirt-clogged throats. Yeoman, holding a scalding mug, went in search of Julia and found her leaning weakly against the remains of a wall. She looked all in, but she smiled as he came up to her.

'You look a bit of a mess,' she said.

He grinned ruefully, looking down at his ruined uniform. 'You don't look so hot yourself,' he retorted. 'God, what a bloody awful mess this all is!'

Suddenly, he reached out and took her by the shoulders.

'Julia,' he said, 'there's something I must tell you. I'm going back to the Squadron. Tonight. It seems all so wrong, continuing my leave when this—this murder is happening. I have to get back. I'm sorry, love. You do understand, don't you?'

For a few moments she made no reply. Then, as though suddenly oblivious to the turmoil around them, she threw herself into his arms and pressed her face to his chest. In a dull, muffled voice, she said:

'I knew you were going to say that. I knew it. Damn you, George, no, I don't understand. But you'll go back anyway, and I won't stop you.'

Suddenly she was weeping bitterly, the pent-up tension flowing from her.

'Oh, George,' she sobbed, 'to hell with everything! The very next time we meet, the *very* next time, get a special licence or whatever it is and marry me. I've had enough...let me be with you, always....'

# Chapter Seven

Yeoman sat in Freddie Barnes' office, catching up with the latest Intelligence reports on Operation Diver, the air defence of southern England against the flying-bomb menace. There was a lot of catching up to be done, too, for events had moved at an alarming pace while he had been away on leave.

The Intelligence summary told him that at 0400 hours on 13 June, a Mosquito crew of 418 Squadron, returning from an intruder operation, had seen what they reported as 'a rocket projectile heading northwards and leaving a red trail'. This had been one of the first salvo of four v-1s launched by the Germans. Six more bombs had been launched during the hours that followed; of the total of ten, the most severe damage was caused by the one which fell at Bethnal Green, London. To divert the defences, a lone Messerschmitt 410 had been sent over the capital and had succeeded in its task very well, because it had got itself shot down.

During the next two days the enemy had launched an estimated 250 flying-bombs, of which 144 had crossed the British coast and seventy-three had reached Greater London. By this time, many anti-aircraft batteries had been moved from the immediate London area and re-located in a series of defensive belts nearer to the coast. Additional units of the Air Defence of Great Britain— fighter squadrons equipped with Tempests, Spitfires, Typhoons, Mustangs and Mosquitos—had also been rushed to forward airfields in Kent and Sussex, from where constant partrols were flown.

Yeoman was elated to learn that it was a Mosquito crew, from 605 Squadron, which had been the first to destroy one of the bombs. They had caught one at low level over the Channel soon after midnight on 15 June and dived after it. The pilot's report was attached to the Intelligence summary.

'It was like chasing a ball of fire across the sky,' Yeoman read. 'It flashed by our starboard side a few thousand feet away at the same height as we were flying. I quickly turned to port and gave chase. It was going pretty fast, but I caught up with it and opened fire from astern. At first, there was no effect so I closed in another hundred yards and gave it another burst. Then I went closer still and pressed the gun button again. This time, there was a terrific flash and explosion and the thing fell down in a vertical dive into the sea. The whole show was over in about three minutes.'

At first sight, shooting down the flying-bombs seemed easy enough, but as Yeoman read further that notion was soon dispelled.

Usually, intercepting pilots had only thirty miles— sometimes considerably less—in which to catch the bombs before they arrived over British territory. The technique developed in the first few days of the v-1 offensive was to patrol at medium altitude and build up speed in a dive once the target was sighted; as the majority of the bombs seemed to fly at about 2,500 feet, at a speed of 350 mph, overtaking them did not prove to be much of a problem.

'Pilots have found considerable difficulty,' the summary went on, 'in judging the vector and distance at which to open fire on these small targets. The problem is particularly acute at night, when the distance between the intercepting fighter and the flame from the tail of the flying-bomb can be very deceptive, and no doubt accounts for the failure of many pilots to hit their target even after several lengthy bursts of fire. Particular importance is attached to finding a solution to this problem, in view of the limited time available to pilots in which to engage the enemy weapons. If a pilot fails to engage a flying-bomb before it reaches the coastal gun belt, he is at once to break off his attack and, if the bomb is not destroyed by the anti-aircraft barrage, he is to engage it again as it passes between the gun belt and the balloon barrage, which is situated immediately to the south of London....'

Doesn't give a chap much of a chance, thought Yeoman. It was obviously essential to get the attack right first time. The question was, how?

His thoughts were interrupted by Tim Sloane, who put his head round the door and grinned. Yeoman's deputy was in good spirits; he had just returned from a Diver patrol, and although he had not sighted any flying-bombs he had caught a Junkers 88 off Dieppe and had shot it blazing on to the French coast.

'Good show, Tim,' Yeoman complimented him, when he had heard the story. He tapped the Intelligence summary with his index finger.

'I've just been reading up the latest developments,' he said. 'Shooting these things down doesn't exactly seem to be a piece of cake.'

Sloane shook his head. 'No,' he agreed, 'it isn't. Some of our chaps have had one or two hair-raising moments this week. Terry Saint bagged our first bomb, and the poor sod got the shock of his life. Apparently he closed right in to fifty yards and flew slap through the middle of the explosion. It stripped the paint completely off his Mosquito and ruined two pairs of underpants!'

Yeoman grinned, then said: 'I see by your initials on the cover that you've read this summary, Tim. How do you see the problem?'

Sloane shrugged. 'Pretty much the same,' he said. 'The bloody things are so small and elusive that you've got to close right in to make certain of a hit, bearing in mind that you've only got a limited amount of time to play with, and then you risk being blown up along with it when it explodes. So far, everybody who has fired at one from 150 yards or less—and that includes myself—has brought back a damaged aircraft, with débris sucked into the radiators and so on. One of 373's crews had to bale out the other night when débris smashed both propellers.'

Yeoman grunted. 'There must be an easier way,' he said. 'We'll have to think hard about this one, Tim.'

He looked at his watch, then got up and locked the Intelligence summary away in a steel cabinet, depositing the key with the duty Intelligence Officer in the next room. Then, accompanied by Sloane, he walked over to the mess for something to eat.

It was seven-thirty in the morning. Strange to think, he reflected, that twenty hours ago he had been grovelling in the ruins of the Guards Chapel, and that it was less than twelve hours since he had said goodbye to Julia.

He did not want to think about that goodbye; the memory of it was too fresh, too painful. He turned his mind sharply away from it, helped by the sight of a flight of Mosquitos returning from patrol, and by Sloane's conversation.

'From what you've seen so far, Tim, what's the best time to catch the flying-bombs?' he asked.

Sloane thought for a moment, then replied: 'Dawn and dusk, I reckon. That's when the big salvoes seem to be launched, probably because they're trying to catch us in the transition period between the day and night fighter patrols. Except it doesn't work like that. Clive Bowen said that he was getting nicely lined up on a bomb the other night when something went past him like a bat out of hell and shot it down; it was a Tempest that had beaten him to it, so the day fighter boys seem very reluctant to go home after dark.'

'What sort of system have you been following?' Yeoman wanted to know. 'Have you been patrolling at fixed times, or as and when required?'

'We've been working very closely with the Mosquito squadrons of 140 Wing at Gravesend,' his companion answered, 'taking turn-and-turn-about with them, so the times have varied a bit, but in general it's been dawn and dusk when we've been most active, We've worked out a system whereby each aircraft patrols its own sector of the French coast at about eight thousand feet, keeping just clear of the coastal flak, and when one of us sees a salvo starting to come up he gives a yell and we all come piling in.'

'Taking yet another leaf out of nature's book,' Yeoman grinned. 'Vultures follow more or less the same principle, or so I understand. They string themselves out over hundreds of square miles of sky, and when one goes down on its prey its neighbours see it descending and go down too, starting a kind of chain reaction.'

Yeoman returned a salute of an airman who was passing, then said:

'Anyway, Tim, you seem to have got things pretty well organized in my absence, and I certainly don't propose to change anything. I'll fly this evening, and look at things for myself.'

They crossed the coast as the sun was setting, the last fragment of its glowing disc nothing more than a sliver of molten gold on the western horizon. Ahead of the Mosquito's nose, dusk had already fallen on the continent of Europe.

Beside Yeoman, Hardy was fiddling with the controls of his AI radar set and swearing quietly to himself. All of 380 Squadron's Mosquitos except two had now been fitted with airborne interception radar, but not with other refinements such as the Serrate equipment in Clive Bowen's night-fighting aircraft, and navigators who were not already qualified in its use had been sent off on the appropriate course two at a time. The AI was going to come in useful in determining the range of the elusive flying-bombs; looking further ahead, when the squadron returned to its task of supporting the Allied ground forces in France, it would also extend the Mosquitos' 'confound and destroy' capability immeasurably, for the Luftwaffe was now operating almost exclusively under cover of darkness.

It was a perfect night, with almost limitless visibility. As he climbed out over the Channel, still a long way from his designated patrol area off Boulogne, Yeoman gave a sudden exclamation, causing Hardy to look up from his radar screen.

Emerging from the spreading darkness over France, like stars which had come down to earth, came a cluster of twinkling lights, moving slowly over the horizon.

'What do you make of them, Happy?' asked Yeoman of his navigator, who had already flown a number of Diver patrols with other pilots during the squadron commander's absence on leave.

'They're chuff bombs all right,' Hardy announced confidently, using the name that was generally coming into use among the defending fighter squadrons to describe the v-1s.

'They're too far up the coast, though,' he observed. 'We wouldn't have a snowball's chance in hell of catching them.'

Yeoman stared at the red, pulsating lights. For the first time, he appreciated the problem other pilots had found in assessing the range between fighters and flying-bombs; the lights might have been two miles away, or a dozen.

The fighters in that particular sector were on to them, though, because a few moments later the R/T was jammed with chatter, clinical and punctilious at first, then becoming more excited as the pilots closed in for the kill.

'One nine, engaging contact to starboard, low.'

'Two two, three more launches observed, heading about three one zero.'

'One nine, attacking.'

'Piss off, he's mine!' The last a frantic yell from

someone to someone else who had got in his way at the last moment.

'Put your bloody nav lights on, then!'

'Dingbat leader to all Dingbat aircraft. Switch on your navigation lights before attacking. And cut the chatter.'

Yeoman grinned as he recognized the Welsh lilt of Clive Bowen's voice. It had a temporary effect on the volume of noise coming over the radio. Then someone said, his voice full of triumph:

'Got the bastard!'

A vivid flash in the northern sky marked the end of one of the flying-bombs.

Suddenly, another cluster of fiery little comets came into view over the French coast. They seemed much closer this time and Yeoman selected the brightest, opening the throttles and purring the Moaquito into a long dive. The note of the Merlins rose to a strident howl as the speed built up.

Over the intercom, Yeoman said: 'Have you got this one on radar, Happy?'

The navigator hesitated for a moment, then replied, 'No...not yet. Lots of sea echoes on the tube...hang on... Yes! There he is blinking in from the right...nicely centred now, range four thousand feet.'

The Mosquito trembled as Yeoman began to level out, slowly overhauling the target and turning in behind it. Face glued to the rubber surround of his cathode ray tube, Hardy chanted out the closing range.

'Two thousand five hundred feet... two thousand feet... one thousand five hundred...'

Yeoman suddenly remembered to switch on his navigation lights as a warning to other fighters in the vicintiy. As he did so, a disgusted voice came clearly over the radio:

'Oh, shit!'

Somebody else had obviously been chasing the same target, but Yeoman was going to get there first.

'One thousand feet, skipper.' An anxious note was

creeping into Hardy's voice as the distance between the Mosquito and the v-1 continued to narrow, The red glare of the bomb's exhaust was centred squarely in the luminous diamonds of Yeoman's reflector sight.

There was no sense in pushing his luck on this first attempt. At three hundred yards range he opened fire, loosing off a short burst with both cannon and machine-guns. Tracer, like glowing, multi-coloured pearls, streaked out into the night and converged on the dark outline of the flying-bomb, clearly visible now against the faint streak of light that still shimmered over the far horizon.

Nothing happened. The v-1 continued steadily on its course. Yeoman took a deep breath and closed the range still further. Hardy had lifted his gaze from the radar set and was now staring through the windscreen, as if paralysed, at the stubwinged, explosive-laden object in front of him.

Yeoman's thumb jabbed down on the firing-button. The bark of the cannon sounded unnaturally loud, like giant hammers beating on a metal drum. The whole cockpit shuddered with the recoil; the breeches of the 20-mms were directly under the floor and the thudding explosions as the shells pumped out transmitted themselves through the thin metal into the feet of the men, making their ankles ache.

Some of the shells found their mark, exploding in a series of twinkling flashes near the flying-bomb's tail. Yeoman and the petrified Hardy tensed, waiting for the bang as the bomb's warhead went off.

It never came. Instead, the glare of the v-1's jet exhaust was suddenly extinguished and the flying-bomb went into wild gyrations, toppling over on a wing-tip and spinning down towards the Channel. Its warhead exploded as it hit the water; there was a brilliant burst of white light, and then the darkness closed in once more.

Hardy wiped the sweat from his forehead and returned to the dancing images on his radar screen.

'Contacts all over the place, skipper. Most of them our fighters. It's getting pretty crowded around here.'

Yeoman gave a non-committal grunt and brought the Mosquito round in a wide turn, searching the sky. A set of navigation lights flashed past on the left, dangerously close, and more slid by a few hundred feet below, heading in the opposite direction.

'You need to have eyes in your arse in the middle of this lot,' Yeoman commented. By the sound of the radio chatter the fighters were having a pretty good time; one after the other, pilots reported the destruction of flying-bombs. But the success was not without its cost; on one occasion, Yeoman heard someone put out a Mayday distress call. Somewhere out there, a Mosquito—thankfully not from his own squadron or Bowen's—was gliding down to a watery landing in the Channel, damaged by débris or explosion.

'Turn on to two-seven-zero and fly straight and level for a minute, skipper, will you?'

Yeoman obediently did as he was told, and a moment later Hardy said:

'Yes, there's a small contact at seven o'clock, range about two miles. Can you see anything?'

The pilot turned his head, peering back over his left shoulder in the direction indicated by Hardy. Almost at once, he spotted another comet-like red glow from a flying-bomb's exhaust. The v-i was flying parallel to them, and Yeoman marvelled yet again at Hardy's astuteness. As soon as he picked up the contact, the navigator's first act had been to turn the Mosquito on to a similar heading so that they could keep pace with it. Their previous chase had brought them quite close to the English coast, and if Hardy had steered the pilot straight towards the v-i they might not have had time to turn in astern and attack it before it reached the gun belt.

'I've got it, Happy,' Yeoman affirmed. 'It's a chuff bomb, all right. Let's hope that some bastard doesn't beat us to it.'

Yeoman fed power to the overworked Merlin engines once more and took the Mosquito racing on a course to intercept the enemy missile. As he came round to position himself for the attack, he misjudged his approach slightly and turned too tightly, with the result that he found himself immediately above the v-1. Swearing at his own error, he weaved from side to side in order to keep the flying-bomb in sight and reduced speed very slightly, waiting for it to pull ahead. The Mosquito was about a thousand feet higher than the v-1, which was flying at fifteen hundred feet, so if it pulled too far ahead he could close the range with a dive.

Yeoman dipped the Mosquito's starboard wing, and Hardy craned his neck in an effort to see the bomb through the side window.

'It's starting to draw ahead now,' he announced, and immediately went back to his radar.

'Tell me when it's nine hundred feet ahead,' the pilot ordered.

The shape of the flying-bomb crept slowly in front of the Mosquito's nose, and for the first time Yeoman was able to study the details of the v-1 almost at leisure. The sleek, shark-like lines of the missile were lit up by the ruddy glow of its own jet exhaust; he was impressed by the brutal simplicity of it, and had to work hard to fight down a sudden irrational feeling that at any moment the thing was going to turn on the Mosquito and attack it with savage, destructive mindlessness. A shiver ran down his spine as he found himself staring into the burning, pulsing cauldron of the jet; it was rather like having a glimpse of hell through a keyhole.

Cautiously, he lost height until the Mosquito was flying in the v-1's trail of hot exhaust gases. The fighter rocked in the turbulence and Yeoman gripped the stick harder, lining up the flying-bomb in his sights. Both the v-1 and its pursuer were travelling at over 350 mph.

'Nine hundred feet,' Hardy announced.

His last word was abruptly drowned by the crash of

the cannon as Yeoman opened fire. The first burst was right on target.

A searing splash of orange light expanded across the sky in the Mosquito's path. There was no time to take evasive action, or even to feel fear. At 350 mph—450 feet per second—they raced into the heart of the fiery storm.

A terrific thud shook the Mosquito and part of the windscreen became opaque. Superheated air and an acrid stench of smoke and burnt metal swept into the cockpit through the ventilator. Glowing fragments, like a blazing snowstorm—if such a thing had been possible—surrounded the fighter for a fraction of a second and then whirled away rearwards, spinning and fading to extinction in the darkness.

Then they were through, virtually blinded by the flash, but still flying. Gradually, their night vision returned.

Hardy let out a sudden yell of alarm that pierced Yeoman's eardrums.

'The nose, skipper! The bloody nose has gone!'

It was an exaggeration, but nevertheless the damage was bad enough. Although it was difficult to ascertain precise details because of the darkness, it looked as though there was a gaping hole in the top of the nose. Fragments of wood broke away and pinged against the cockpit canopy. The Mosquito shuddered violently and Yeoman hastily throttled back, reducing the airspeed to 150 mph and lowering ten degrees of flap. This had the effect of raising the nose a little, reducing the volume of air that was buffeting into the damaged section.

'Radar's packed in, skipper,' Hardy announced. 'Scanner must have taken a hell of a bang.'

'So has the radio,' Yeoman said. 'Aerials torn away by débris, probably. Everything else seems to be all right, though. Still, we'd better get down somewhere as soon as we can. What's the nearest airfield, Happy?'

The navigator checked his map in the dim blue glow of his light. 'Lympne', he said a moment later, naming an airfield near Folkestone. 'Steer three-five-five.'

Yeoman peered out of the cockpit. The coast of Kent was on his left; flying-bombs must still be crossing it en route to London, for the anti-aircraft guns were putting up a fearsome barrage and the sky was lurid with searchlight beams. Some miles ahead of the Mosquito's nose, the vague dark outline of a broad spit of land jutted out into the Channel.

'I can see Dungeness,' Yeoman said. 'That's the beginning of one of the fighter entry lanes, isn't it?'

The fighter entry lanes were narrow 'corridors' leading through the anti-aircraft belt. Any Allied aircraft coming into south-east England at any other point while an alert was on risked being blown out of the sky, especially if it was flying fast and at low level.

'Yes,' agreed Hardy. 'Hold your present heading for the time being and turn in when I tell you.'

'You'd better get ready to fire some recognition signals, just in case,' Yeoman told the navigator. 'What are the colours of the day?'

'Red-white-red,' Hardy said, and reached up for the signal pistol, which was located on the roof behind the pilot's head. The signal cartridges were clipped to the front of the navigator's own seat.

'All right, skipper, turn in now. Two-eight-zero degrees. And start praying. If somebody down there gets trigger-happy, they aren't likely to miss us at this altitude.'

Yeoman glanced at the altimeter; the Mosquito was down to a thousand feet. The navigator reached out a hand and flicked on the air recognition lights switch, on the starboard side of the cockpit. Lit up like a Christmas tree, the Mosquito turned in towards the coast.

After a minute, Hardy said: 'That's Dymchurch below, We're okay. Keep going until you see the Ashford—Folkestone railway-line, then turn right on to one-one-zero degrees. Should bring us nicely into the circuit.'

A searchlight probed up towards them, followed by

another, and Yeoman raised a hand to shield his eyes from the intense blue-white glare.

'Better shoot off some flares, Happy,' he instructed.

Hardy repositioned the flare pistol in its aperture and fired off the recognition signals in quick succession. The searchlights wavered, then flicked out.

'That's better,' Hardy muttered, passing a hand over his eyes. 'Can't see a bloody thing now, though.'

'That's all right,' Yeoman said. 'I can see Lympne already. The flarepath's lit. Stand by to flash the lights as soon as I join the circuit.'

Yeoman brought the Mosquito cautiously into the downwind leg of the aerodrome circuit, lowering the undercarriage and keeping a careful lookout for other navigation lights to make sure that no one was below or ahead of him. On his command Hardy flashed the identification lights steadily on and off to indicate to the airfield controller their urgent need to land. The urgency, in fact, was becoming greater with every break away from the aircraft's damaged nose.

There was no answering signal from the ground.

'Give 'em a white flare,' the pilot ordered. Hardy swiftly complied, and a white Verey signal light arced away from the Mosquito, falling slowly towards the ground. A few moments later, a green light flashed from the control tower.

'About bloody time, too,' the pilot muttered, and brought the Mosquito round on to final approach. The Merlins popped and crackled as he throttled back over the runway threshold and then the aircraft was down, settling on its sturdy undercarriage.

A light utility car came out to meet the Mosquito as it came to the end of its landing run. Mounted on the vehicle was the illuminated 'follow me' sign.

The car led Yeoman round the perimeter track to a dispersal. He shut down the engines, switched off the electrical services and followed Hardy out of the cockpit, taking a deep breath of the warm night air.

They both stepped back a few yards, took a long look at the Mosquito and swallowed hard. Apart from the damage to the nose, in which a great chunk of metal from the v-i was later found to be embedded, the aircraft was scorched and scarred as though a giant blow-torch had swept over it. Yeoman shuddered. 'It looks bad enough even in this light,' he said. 'I hate to think what it'll look like in the morning. Come on, Happy, let's go and find ourselves a cup of tea. I reckon we've earned it.'

# Chapter Eight

The battle against the flying-bombs went on unabated by day and night. Considerable numbers of the missiles were shot down, but the airborne explosion of their warheads and flying débris continued to be a problem.

Then, on 23 June—three days after Yeoman's close shave—a Spitfire pilot ran out of ammunition while attacking a V-1. In sheer frustration, seeing the bomb fly steadily on, he closed in alongside it and eased the wing-tip of his fighter under that of the missile. The airflow caused the V-1 to roll, toppling the gyroscope that stabilized it, and it plunged down to explode harmlessly in open country.

From now on, this became the recommended method of destroying the flying-bombs. It needed a steady hand and a cool nerve, but it worked, although some pilots still preferred to take the risk and shoot the V-1s down by more orthodox methods. During July, 380 Squadron, on average, shot down (or sent out of control) one flying-bomb a day, and the score of their sister squadron, 373, was something similar. In the beginning, shooting down a V-1 had not counted as an air-to-air victory which could be added to a pilot's personal score, on the basis that the robot bombs could not really fight back; but in July the Air Ministry relented and a V-1 destroyed over the sea counted as one kill, while one destroyed over land counted as half a kill. This was supposed to give pilots added incentive to knock the bombs down before they reached the coast.

Then, towards the end of July, the V-1 battle took a

new turn. On the twenty-fifth—five days after the astonishing news had leaked out that an attempt had been made on Hitler's life by some of his generals—four flying-bombs approached London from the north-east, in other words, from the North Sea.

There could only be one possible explanation: the bombs had been launched from aircraft. This was a serious threat, for it meant that no objective in Britain—none, at any rate, that was in range of the Luftwaffe's bombers—was safe from attack. It didn't take a mathematician to work out that V-IS launched from German bombers several miles off the east coast of England could reach the industrial towns of the Midlands.

Within twenty-four hours the Mosquito squadrons were on their way back from Tangmere to Burningham in a move to counter the new menace. They flew northwards in formation, landed in the early evening, and flew their first patrols that same night, probing out towards Holland and Belgium.

They saw nothing; but several flying-bombs crossed East Anglia en route to the capital, so the launch aircraft must have been there.

'This is bloody ridiculous,' said a weary Yeoman to Clive Bowen as they ate their breakfast after returning from their patrol.

'We could go on like this for weeks, chasing up and down the North Sea. It's obvious that they're coming in flat on the deck, so there's no chance of our ground radar stations spotting them, and even if we locate them with our airborne gear—well, it's difficult enough to shoot down an aircraft that's flying over water by day, let alone at night. You're concentrating so much on not going into the drink that you haven't time to get lined up properly.'

Bowen agreed entirely. 'And if we miss them,' he said, 'the chances are that they'll get through—the bombs, I mean. There's just no possibility of extending the gun belt all the way up the east coast.'

Yeoman cradled his mug of tea between his hands and

looked thoughtfully at his table companion.

'The answer, I suppose, is to clobber them on their airfields, if we can find out where they are operating from. But I'd like to bet that the crafty bastards are dispersed in ones and twos all over Holland and Belgium. If we could extend our radar coverage a bit it would help.'

'What about a fighter director ship, like they used during the invasion?' said Bowen. 'If one was positioned, say, twenty miles off the Schelde Estuary, its radar could almost certainly pick up anything crossing the Dutch coast. At least we'd know then where to start looking.'

Yeoman gave a grunt. 'It might work,' he admitted. 'We've got to get something organized, though. We've had one wasted night, and we can't afford many more. The whole thing is far too hit-and-miss. Anyway, I'm off to grab a couple of hours' sleep and then I'll pop along to Intelligence to see if Freddie Barnes has any more gen for us.'

Yeoman found Barnes in a gloomy mood. The Intelligence Officer looked at him and said:

'You aren't going to like this. I've just had word that a few hours after you left Tangmere, quite a large force of enemy aircraft—Dornier 217s and Heinkel 177s, we believe—attacked shipping in Portsmouth and Southampton harbours with radio-controlled glider bombs. They caused quite a bit of damage, and all but one of them got clean away. They attacked after dark, so there wasn't much the day fighter boys could do. It would have been a different story if the two Mossie squadrons had still been at Tangmere, though, as it's just up the road from Portsmouth.'

'Damn!' Yeoman swore. 'You'd almost think that they knew we had gone.'

'They probably did,' Barnes said wryly. 'No doubt they still have plenty of agents operating in and around the south coast ports. Then, of course, there's Nosey Joe.'

'Nosey Joe' was the nickname, probably of American

origin, that had been bestowed on an enemy reconnaissance aircraft which flew over the south coast twice a day, morning and evening, as regularly as clockwork. It came over very high, at least 45,000 feet, and nothing could get near it. It was very fast and clearly jet-propelled; probably one of the new Arado 234s which were rumoured to be based at Juvincourt, near Reims.

'Yes,' Yeoman agreed, 'it's time something was done about that so-and-so. Anyway, Freddie, now that you've given me the bad news and cheered me up no end, what have you got on these bomb-launching Huns?'

Barnes looked worried and polished his thick horn-rimmed glasses, as he always did when called upon to make an Intelligence assessment. He really had no need to be nervous, for he had an uncanny ability to see through a tangle of conjecture and pick out the few probable facts, piecing them together like a jigsaw puzzle.

'Well,' said Barnes, 'we think they are Heinkel 111s and that they belong to KG 54—the Luftwaffe's 54th Bomber Wing. They were based in Holland until the end of June, then they suddenly disappeared off the scene until last week, when they were reported to have returned. The likelihood is that they were withdrawn for modifications so as to be able to carry the flying-bombs.'

'Where are they?' Yeoman wanted to know.

'Ah,' the Intelligence Officer answered, shaking his head, 'that's the problem. They came back to their former base at Gilze, but now they've disappeared again. We think they've dispersed to other airfields in the Low Countries, but we don't know for sure.'

'Blast,' Yeoman muttered, 'that means we can't clobber them all in one go. We'll just have to think of something else, that's all.'

In the meantime, there was little they could do except patrol the North Sea constantly between dusk and dawn, hoping to catch the elusive Heinkels as they slipped over at wave-top height before they popped up to launch their v-1s. Yeoman, Bowen and Wing Commander Bentley, the OC Flying, worked out a system whereby the Mosquitos would patrol in relays of six, strung out in a line between the Hook of Holland and the coast of East Anglia. In this way, even if one of the night fighters made contact with an enemy bomber and then lost it again, the theory was that its approximate heading and speed could be passed on to the next fighter in line, which would hopefully pick it up on its AI radar and intercept it. Each night-fighter crew was briefed to fly a leg of a hundred miles, turning through 180 degrees and flying on a reciprocal course at each end. It would be boring and monotonous work, but it was hoped that it would produce results.

It did—as far as locating the German bombers was concerned. But shooting them down turned out to be quite another matter, as Sergeant Martinsen—380 Squadron's Norwegian pilot—discovered to his cost.

Shortly after 0130 in the morning of 28 July, Martinsen's navigator picked up a strong contact heading out from the Dutch coast and steered his pilot in pursuit. Martinsen manoeuvred until he was dead astern and identified the enemy aircraft as a Heinkel 111, but it was flying so low that he could not depress the nose of his Mosquito enough to get the bomber in his sight. He climbed with a view to making a diving attack, but as soon as he did so the radar 'blip' of the Heinkel became lost in the sea clutter on the cathode ray tube and it was some minutes before his navigator managed to locate it again.

The next ten minutes were the most unnerving Martinsen had ever spent. Several times he closed in to within firing range, but the German pilot was no beginner and each time he sent the Heinkel skidding and swerving over the sea, his wing-tips brushing the water, so that the bomber kept sliding out of Martinsen's sights. Once, in sheer frustration, Martinsen opened fire, but his tracers flickered harmlessly over the target and the Heinkel escaped unharmed.

Beside Martinsen, sweating with fear, one eye on the AI
103

radar and the other on the radar altimeter, his navigator tensed every muscle in anticipation of a brutal impact with the water. Black waves, capped with white, streamed under the Mosquito's wings at terrifying speed, so close it seemed almost possible to reach down and touch them.

Suddenly, unexpectedly, the Heinkel began to climb.

'We've got him!' Martinsen yelled. 'We've got the bastard!'

The silhouette of the Heinkel was clearly visible, hanging in the night sky a few hundred yards ahead. Martinsen could even make out the dark, sinister shape of the flying-bomb, suspended under the bomber's port wing.

An instant later, a vivid orange glare burst through the darkness, closely followed by a string of Norwegian oaths. Momentarily blinded, Martinsen instinctively opened the throttles and pulled back the stick, sending the Mosquito bounding skywards. His navigator, intent on calling out the range by reference to his radar screen, was taken by surprise; his stomach, already rebelling against the low-level turbulence through which the Mosquito had been buffeting, finally gave up the struggle and he threw up all over the instrument panel, tearing aside his face mask just in time.

Martinsen realized at once what had happened. The Heinkel had pulled up to launch its flying-bomb and it was the glare of its igniting motor that had blinded him.

As soon as he had gained enough height, he put the Mosquito into level flight, still swearing and waiting for his night vision to return. He looked across at his navigator, who was retching weakly.

'Sorry about that, Harry,' he said, 'Are you okay?'

The navigator nodded miserably, wiping his mouth with the back of his hand. Clipping his face mask back into place, he bent over his cathode ray tube once more. For several minutes he carried out a fruitless search, but the Heinkel had vanished.

'Oh, well,' said Martinsen, 'we lost him, and that's

that. You have to admit that the Hun pilot had plenty of guts. I wouldn't have sat there for fifteen minutes with a Mossie on my tail.'

When Martinsen returned to base and made his report, he discovered that one of 373 Squadron's pilots had had a similar experience. The Heinkel had clung doggedly to its course until it was almost within sight of the British coast and had then launched its v-i, whose bright engine exhaust had blinded the pursuer for long enough to enable the bomber to make its escape.

Yeoman summed it up. 'We're going to have to get 'em as close as possible to the Dutch coast,' he said. 'The question is, how?'

A possible solution arrived suddenly at Burningham at the end of the first week in August in the shape of a black-painted Vickers Wellington. As soon as it arrived, it was tucked away inconspicuously in a far corner of the airfield and an armed guard placed around it.

The Wellington, it transpired, came from the Telecommunications Research Establishment's flying unit at Defford in Worcestershire, and its presence at Burningham was the result of much string-pulling behind the scenes by Wing Commander Bentley, who had a nameless but clearly very senior contact at TRE.

The Wellington's outline was marred by a host of protruding radio aerials and an enormous radome fitted under the nose, which quickly earned the aircraft the nickname of 'The Pregnant Wimpey'. It was, in fact, an airborne radar control station, and had been used operationally for a short time during the D-Day landings before returning to Defford for further modifications.

With its help, Bentley hoped that the Burningham Wing would at last be in a position to come to grips with the air-launched v-1 threat.

The procedure looked simple enough. The Wellington would cruise high over the North Sea, flying a fixed pattern off the Dutch coast, and its airborne search radar would pick up the Heinkels as they took off from their bases; the controller on board would then steer the night fighers into a favourable position to carry out an interception.

Eight Mosquitos, spread out at intervals, accompanied the Wellington on its first trip; Yeoman and Hardy were in one of them. They had been on patrol for just over half an hour when the Wellington made its first radar contact. Yeoman pricked up his ears as the controller's voice came over the R/T, but the message was directed at one of the other aircraft.

'Black Ball Five, this is Fisher. Have a contact for you. Steer one-six-zero. Target range is one zero miles, speed one-five-zero, course two-six-zero.'

'Black Ball Five, Roger, one-six-zero.'

The voice that answered was Terry Saint's.

'That young beggar gets all the luck,' Hardy grunted over the intercom. 'If he fell down a sewer, he'd come up wearing a pearl necklace.'

Yeoman listened to the radio exchange between Saint and the radar controller as the New Zealander closed on his target.

'Black Ball Five, make your heading now one-eight-zero; the range is five miles.'

The controller was bringing Saint into position for a stern attack on the enemy aircraft. Yeoman could imagine Saint's navigator, glued to his A1 set, eagerly awaiting the first sign of the elusive 'blip'. He must have found it, because a few moments later Saint reported that contact had been made. The controller in the Wellington, his job done for the time being, wished him good luck. Everything was now up to the team whose call-sign was Black Ball Five.

'Tally-ho!' Saint's call came faintly over the radio. The seconds ticked by. Then, to the south-east, something flared low down on the horizon and was almost immediately extinguished.

The radio was silent. Yeoman pressed the transmit button and called:

'Black Ball Five, this is Black Ball One. Did you get that Hun?'

There was no answer. Yeoman tried again, and this time, distorted and strange, little more than a whisper, he heard Saint acknowledge his call.

'We got him...we have some trouble. I think...stand by.'

Yeoman waited for a couple of minutes, then called Saint again. No answering voice broke through the hiss and crackle of static.

Then there was no longer any time to worry about the fate of Black Ball Five, for suddenly the controller's terse voice came on the air again:

'Black Ball One, this is Fisher, contact for you range five miles, course two-six-five, speed one-six-zero. Steer one-seven-zero to intercept,'

Yeoman brought the Mosquito round sharply. Hardy bent over his A1 set, muttering: 'How the hell did I miss that one?'

He picked up the glowing blip on his cathode ray tube almost at once, and said urgently: 'He's crossing from left to right, skipper, range about fifteen thousand feet now. Keep the turn going and roll out on two-six-zero—and can you increase the speed a bit, please, or I'll lose him in the clutter.'

Yeoman did as he was bidden, sweeping low across the sea as Hardy chanted out the diminishing range. At two thousand feet he located the target visually; it was a Heinkel all right, complete with v-1, and it was flying very slowly under the drag of its burden.

Yeoman throttled back as much as he dared until the Mosquito was hanging on its propellers just above stalling speed, a hundred feet over the water. It was a dangerous manoeuvre, but he had no intention of overshooting.

'One thousand feet, skipper,' Hardy announced calmly.

Yeoman opened fire, aiming for the Heinkel's starboard wing, away from the highly-explosive v-1. His first burst produced a brief red glow, which went out at once. The bomber began to weave gently from side to side and tracers floated towards him from the turret on top of its fuselage, zipping like meteorites over the top of the Mosquito's cockpit.

He opened the throttles slightly to reduce the range and fired again. This time, the flash of exploding cannon shells lit up the white-edged cross on the bomber's fuselage.

'Don't get too close, skipper,' Hardy warned, Yeoman ignored him and reduced the range still further. At 150 feet he gave the bomber a two-second burst with both cannon and machine-guns; more flashes appeared, this time at the wingroot, and suddenly a garish yellow flame shot back, licking past the Heinkel's tail, growing until it enveloped the whole of the bomber's rear fuselage.

The Heinkel's nose went down and it dived into the sea. There was no explosion. The Mosquito sped over the spot and Yeoman pulled up in a climbing turn, looking down; a patch of foam, whitely phosphorescent in the night, marked the bomber's grave.

Between them, the Mosquitos of Nos 380 and 373 Squadrons destroyed six Heinkels on that August night, all of them before they could launch their flying-bombs. It seemed, at last, that the solution had been found. But Terry Saint and his navigator would not be coming back.

# Chapter Nine

It was the first day of September 1944, and each night, with the approach of autumn, an earlier darkness crept perceptibly over the land.

Five years to the day after German tanks had stormed into Poland and precipitated the greatest and bloodiest conflict in the history of the world, the darkness was already closing in fast on the Thousand-Year Reich.

In July, during the weeks following the invasion, there had been virtual stalemate on the western front; but the Allies had steadily consolidated their foothold on the soil of France and poured fresh divisions and supplies into the beachhead. When the breakout finally came, in August, it came with shattering speed that spelt the end of the German cause in Normandy.

On 12 August, in a desperate attempt to save their divisions from annihilation by the Anglo-Canadian forces in the east and the Americans in the west, the Germans had begun to fall back through the Argentan-Falaise Gap. Three days later, nearly a quarter of a million men were in chaotic retreat along a corridor forty miles long and eleven miles wide, battered on three flanks and subjected to a merciless round-the-clock onslaught from the air.

Twenty-two squadrons of Typhoons and Spitfires of the 2nd Tactical Air Force turned the Falaise Gap into a killing ground. The Typhoons would go in first, sealing off the front and rear of an enemy column with accurate bombing, and then make rocket and cannon attacks on the rest. As soon as the Typhoons departed, their place would be taken by Spitfires, making low-level strafing attacks on trucks and lightly armoured vehicles of all kinds.

The Luftwaffe was absent from the sky, and the fighter-bombers turned the retreat into a rout.

By 20 August, when the Allied armies finally sealed the gap in a huge pincer movement, the German Seventh Army had virtually ceased to exist. Eight infantry and two panzer divisions had been wiped out by the awful effectiveness of the air attacks; fifty thousand dazed and bewildered prisoners marched off to captivity, and among the forty-mile swath of smashed and burning vehicles lay ten thousand corpses. Field Marshal Montgomery's strategy had succeeded; there would be no bitter step-by-step slogging match across France, for the prospect of a German fighting retreat had been destroyed forever in Normandy.

In the south, too, the German forces—stripped of men and material in a belated attempt to reinforce those in Normandy—were in full retreat, pursued up the valley of the Rhone by the US Seventh Army and units of the Fighting French, who had landed on the Riviera on 15 August. Eventually, the push from the south would link up with the American drive from the west, while the British and Canadians thrust up the northern flank into Belgium and Holland.

On the eastern front, too, the German military structure was falling apart. The Russian armies were in Romania, and Germany's former allies were collapsing or changing sides; in the north, the Finns were already suing for peace.

In August alone, the RAF and USAAF had dropped 140,000 tons of bombs between them, aiming mainly for the destruction of Germany's dwindling centres of oil production. No modern war machine could function without oil, and in the latter half of 1944 the Allied air attacks, coupled with the loss of the Romanian oilfields, meant that the Germans were growing desperately short of this vital commodity.

In the Pacific, the Americans were rolling back across the islands and preparing to invade the Philippines, while huge B-29 Superfortresses, operating from bases in China, had begun to attack the Japanese Home Islands, heralding the devastating fire-raids that were to follow.

For the enemy, there would be no concessions, no armistice. The only terms would be unconditional surrender. But that was a matter for the politicians; for the men fighting the war on land, at sea and in the air the end was still a long way off, and life was still measured only from one day to the next.

'If only I could be there,' said Yves Romilly wistfully. 'If only I could be there now! Imagine the scenes, the rejoicing, the wine and the women…ah, *mon Dieu*, that I should miss such a moment of history!' He gave a deep sigh, and took a long drink.

Paris had been liberated exactly a week earlier, and Romilly had talked of little else since. It was understandable, for the Frenchman had not seen his home capital since 1939, and he had relatives there about whose fate he knew nothing.

Yeoman smiled at him. 'Cheer up, Yves,' he said, 'I've told you, you'll have your chance soon enough. You'll see Paris at the right time, after all the fuss has died down. There's no use going there now; you're wearing the wrong uniform. I've a feeling the Americans will have the pick of everything, just at the moment.'

Romilly squared his shoulders and glared at his commanding officer.

'Americans?' He waved his arms excitedly. 'Americans—bah! It was General Leclerc's Second Armoured Division, the Fighting French, that liberated Paris!'

'Only because the Americans allowed them to,' Yeoman retorted. 'And if you don't stop waving your arms about, you're likely to spill your beer. Come on, drink up and let's have another.'

On this Friday evening, all the officers of the two Burningham squadrons had been invited across to the sergeants' mess, where a party of appalling proportions was developing. It had started off as a 'Happy Hour', which was supposed to have lasted from 1730 to 1830, but it was now eight o'clock and things were livelier than ever.

The squadrons deserved to let their hair down, thought Yeoman, looking round at the sea of laughing, high-spirited young men. They had done well over the past weeks, chalking up a combined score of eighteen Heinkels, all of them v-1 carriers and all of them at night. In the end, the enemy bombers had ceased to venture out over the North Sea; the Mosquitos had won their battle.

A few flying-bombs, launched from sites in France, still purred over London, but the total was diminishing daily, and as the Allies pushed up the coast towards Belgium the v-1 offensive was slowly petering out. It was a tribute to the defences that, of nearly eleven thousand flying-bombs launched, only 2,400 had got through to their targets; but these had killed 6,200 people and seriously injured 18,000 more, ninety per cent of them in London.

Once again, Londoners had shown that they could take it; but in a strange way, the robot bombs had come closer to destroying morale than the great Blitz of 1940. The deprivations of five years of war had taken their toll, both physically and mentally.

For 380 Squadron, the fight against the flying-bombs was over. Clive Bowen and his 373 Squadron were to remain at Burningham as an insurance against possible further attacks by bomb-launching Heinkels, but Yeoman's Mosquitos had been ordered to move back to 83 Group.

Their new base was to be Carpiquet, on the outskirts of Caen. They were to be one of the first Mosquito squadrons to operate from French territory, and they were to resume their original role of 'search and destroy', carrying out low-level precision attacks on Luftwaffe airfields or on selected targets held to be of particular importance by Intelligence. After weeks of constant patrolling in the dark, far from the focus of the battle in France, all the aircrew were anticipating the move with more than the usual eagerness.

Freddie Barnes pushed his way unsteadily through the throng of blue uniforms, his eyes slightly more glazed than usual behind his spectacle lenses and the tip of his nose a bright red. He beamed at Yeoman and Romilly and stood there without saying anything, swaying slightly and periodically slopping little cascades of beer down the front of his uniform.

'Freddie,' Yeoman said, eyeing the Intelligence Officer with mock severity, 'you are drunk.'

'Sir,' Barnes replied, peering at Yeoman over the top of his glasses, 'so are you. And you, sir'—he addressed Romilly—'have got two pairs of eyes. In fact, you have two pairs of everything. Very dangerous medical condition. Should see the MO, if I were you.'

He weaved away in the direction of the piano and was seized by a group of pilots, who placed him without ceremony on the stool. Warrant Officer Arthur Laurie's bellow silenced the babble of conversation.

'Hey, you guys, knock it off! Freddie's going to hit the keys!'

In the temporary hush, Barnes waved his arms dramatically and said:

'It just so happens that I have penned a little ditty to mark this aus-aus-auspicious occasion.'

'What's horse piss got to do with it?' someone yelled. Barnes turned on the offender and glared at him.

'Silence, peasant, lest the earth rise up and smite thee,' he quoted biblically. 'Now, here goes. Join in the chorus.'

His fingers caressed the keys and, in a rich and
113

surprisingly tuneful baritone, he began to sing:

'From the far north to the Channel,
They have heard our plaintive cry
In the boozers of this land we love so well;
As we drunken sods assemble with our glasses raised
on high,
And the murmur of our voices raising hell....'

Amid roars of approval Barnes launched into the rest
of his repertoire, abruptly changing the tune and the
song.

'Oh, Three-Eighty Squadron's a pretty good place
But the organization's a bloody disgrace!
There's pilots and navs and there's engineers too
With their hands in their pockets and sod all to do!'

Suddenly, in the short pause between verses, a new
voice intervened, The tune was the same, but the words
were different. Yeoman craned his neck, peering through
the haze of tobacco smoke in an effort to locate the
singer.

'They say in the Air Force a landing's okay
If the pilot can get out and still walk away;
But in the Fleet Air Arm the prospects are grim
If the landing's piss-poor and the pilot can't swim!'

A bearded naval officer stood in the doorway, grinning
hugely. On the sleeves of his tunic was the gold braid of
a lieutenant-commander. Yeoman recognized him immediately and let out a yell.

'Russ! Russell Kemp! Over here!'

The newcomer saw Yeoman's upraised hand and pushed his way through the crowd, Shaking Yeoman by the
hand, he said matter-of-factly:

'Hello, George. It's nice to see you.'

'You too, Russ. It's been a long time. By the way, this is Yves Romilly. Russ Kemp and I,' he said by way of explanation to the Frenchman, 'served together in North Africa and Crete back in forty-one.'

Romilly looked from one to the other and shook his head slowly.

'You British,' he said, 'never cease to astonish me. Good friends who have not seen one another for years meet again, and they greet each other as though they travel to work on the same train every morning.'

'Well,' grinned Yeoman, 'you might fancy being kissed on both cheeks by a bearded wonder, but I don't.' He waved to attract the barman's attention, then said to Kemp:

'Seriously, Russ, this is one hell of a surprise. What brings you here?'

'I'm on my way from Hatston, in the Orkneys, to Boscombe Down,' Kemp replied. 'I heard you were here, so I thought I'd stop off and find out how life was treating you. There's an RAF type in flying control at Hatston who knows you, a chap called O'Rourke, or O'Grady, or something like that. Bit of a weird type, if you ask me. Do you remember him?'

'Oh, yes,' said Yeoman, 'I remember him all right. I had him taken off operations last year. O'Grady's the name. He had the "twitch" rather badly and tried to do away with himself. A thorough bloody nuisance.'

Yeoman took a pint of beer from the barman and handed it to Kemp, who swallowed half of it thirstily. Romilly, realizing that the two men wished to reminisce, went off to talk to Tim Sloane, who had just joined the group around the piano.

'Your pianist seems to be in good form,' Kemp smiled. His companion nodded.

'That, believe it or not, is our Intelligence Officer, Freddie Barnes. I didn't know he had it in him.'

By this time, the singers had worked their way through 'Cats on the Rooftops' and were now launching into

'There Was an Old Monk of Great Renown'. The noise was fearsome, and Yeoman shouted into Kemp's ear:

'Come on, let's escape for a few minutes. We'll take our beer into the anteroom.'

The only occupant in the sergeants' mess anteroom was the station warrant officer, who looked up as Yeoman and Kemp came in.

'Good evening, Mr Wallace,' Yeoman said. 'Do you mind if we share your little oasis of peace and quiet for a while?'

The swo, an elderly and much decorated veteran with a quarter of a century of RAF service behind him, smiled.

'Not at all, gentlemen. Make yourselves at home. I'm getting a bit too old for parties, myself.' He buried himself behind his newspaper once more.

Kemp and Yeoman settled themselves in two arm-chairs at the far end of the room; the naval officer looked round appreciatively.

'Very cosy,' he said. 'Better than your officers' mess, in fact. It's as dead as a doornail over there; I was just about reconciled to an evening of lonely drinking when one of the stewards said you were all over here.'

'Well, Russ, you arrived just in time, because we're leaving for France tomorrow,' Yeoman told him. He looked at Kemp in curiosity, and asked: 'What exactly are you up to at the moment?'

'At the moment,' Kemp said, 'I'm taking a Barracuda down to the Armament Experimental Establishment for trials with a new kind of torpedo. Actually, I've got nothing to do with that side of it; I'm starting a few days' leave, so I said I'd deliver the thing. It seemed the quickest way to get near the London fleshpots,' he grinned.

'Are you on a Barracuda squadron now?' Yeoman wanted to know. Kemp looked at him, aghast.

'Good God, no,' he said. 'The Barracuda's a horrible bloody thing—an absolute bag of nails. No, George, I'm still a fighter boy—my squadron has just re-equipped with the Fairey Firefly. A nice piece of work, with an elliptical wing like the Spitfire, a big Griffon engine and four cannon. We used 'em during the attack on the *Tirpitz* last July.'

Yeoman's interest was awakened. 'You were on the *Tirpitz* show, were you? That must have been pretty hairy.' The pocket battleship *Tirpitz* had been lurking in various Norwegian fjords since the autumn of 1943, and as she presented a serious threat to the Allied convoys to Russia several attempts were made to destroy her.

'You can say that again,' Kemp agreed. 'We've been attacking that bloody battleship since last April, and we've still got nowhere. We caused a bit of damage to her superstructure, but the trouble is that the bombs are too small—the heaviest the Barracuda can carry is 1,600 lbs, and they make no impression at all on the ship's heavy armour. We didn't hit her at all in the July attacks, because the Huns knew we were coming and put up a smokescreen around her.

'The only thing that would knock her out,' he went on thoughtfully, 'would be these new "earthquake" bombs the RAF have been dropping on U-boat pens and so on. Yes, that would do the trick all right.'

He paused and looked at Yeoman, giving a small and rather weary smile.

'Sorry, George,' he apologized, 'I seem to be doing nothing but talk about myself. What about you? Did you ever hear from that girl—you know, the one you were always talking about?'

Yeoman laughed. 'Oh, you mean Julia. Yes, we saw each other just a few weeks ago. As a matter of fact, we're thinking about getting married. She's out of the country at the moment on some sort of assignment—I think I may have told you that she's a newspaper correspondent—but she'll be back early in October and we've arranged to meet in London on the seventh, which is her birthday, come hell or high water. I'll be tour-expired by then, anyway, with some leave due to me.'

'So it sounds as though 7 October could be decision time for my old mate George Yeoman,' Kemp smiled. 'I never thought I'd see the day when you were trapped by a female. It'll put an awful curb on your drinking habits, you know.'

'Well, that might not be a bad thing,' Yeoman replied. 'I take it you're still single?'

Kemp nodded. 'Oh, yes. There is a girl in Devon, but...well, I don't feel like committing myself while there's still a war on. Later, maybe. In the meantime, I shall adhere strictly to the tradition of the Navy.'

'What's that?' Yeoman asked.

'Rum, bum and dominoes!'

'I'd like to bet Nelson didn't invent that one,' laughed Yeoman. 'Anyway, what's in store for you now—more attcks on the *Tirpitz*?'

Kemp shook his head. 'No. I think not.' He leaned forward in his chair and said quietly: 'We're going to the Far East, George. *Victorious*, *Indomitable* and *Illustrious* are already out at Ceylon, and my own carrier, the *Indefatigable*, is leaving to join them in a couple of weeks' time. We're going to form a new task force to operate alongside the Americans in the Pacific.'

Yeoman raised his eyebrows. 'Now that sounds like an interesting job of work,' he said. 'One thing I have always regretted is that I never got out to the Far East. Mind you, it can't have been much fun in the early days, with the Japs shooting our blokes out of the sky like flies.'

'No,' Kemp agreed, 'and if we'd had the equipment then that we've got now, it wouldn't have happened. The tragic, bloody part of it is that we could have had it right at the start of the war, if it hadn't been for a lot of purblind politicians in the early thirties. Well, I hope they've learned their lesson. "If you wish for peace, prepare for war." I can't remember who said that, but it had better be the motto of this country from now on.'

'I wonder when it'll all end, Russ,' Yeoman said thoughtfully. 'This war, I mean.'

Kemp shrugged. 'I've a feeling there's a long way to go yet,' he answered. 'Another year, at least, out in the Pacific. Invading Japan is going to be a murderous bloody business; from what I've heard, the Japs would rather be annihilated than surrender.'

Yeoman nodded soberly. 'God,' he said, 'there are going to be some pieces to pick up when this lot's over, and no mistake.'

Both men were silent for a few moments; then Yeoman got up suddenly and slapped Kemp on the shoulder.

'To hell with it, Russ,' he said, 'this conversation is getting too deadly serious. Let's go and have another beer or six.'

They went back to the noise and smoke of the bar, circumventing a mass of tangled bodies in the middle of the floor where an impromptu game of rugby was in full swing. Freddie Barnes was still at the piano, playing to a dwindling audience; his glasses now hung from one ear and his eyes were slightly crossed.

Clive Bowen rose from the scrum, shedding two sergeants and a flying officer, and yelled: 'George, you old bastard! Where've you been? I've been trying to buy you a drink all evening.'

Yeoman introduced Kemp to 373 Squadron's burly commander and the three of them headed for the bar. Bowen got the drinks, then raised his glass to Yeoman and said quietly:

'Well, George, we've been a good team between us, this past year. I wish we were coming with you.'

'So do I, Clive,' Yeoman answered. 'So do I.'

That was the way it always was, he reflected sadly. Shared dangers turned total strangers into good friends; they fought alongside you, lived and played alongside you, and sometimes died alongside you, and then the demands of war one day sent the living on their separate ways. There were inevitable promises of keeping in touch, but one seldom did; paths sometimes crossed again, but such encounters were usually accidental. To

Yeoman, an unexpected meeting with old friends such as Russ Kemp and Jim Callender was a source of vast pleasure; but always, deep down, was the pain of knowing that the meeting might be for the last time.

Paradoxically, wartime was the best, and yet the worst of times in which to form close friendships. It brought greater value, greater trust. But often, when friends departed, it was better to leave it there; better, in the long run, not to know what had become of them.

# Chapter Ten

The ancient town of Caen was a shambles. Yeoman had never seen anything like it: not in Tobruk, nor Malta, nor anywhere. Together with Hardy and Tim Sloane, he stood beside the ruins of what had once been a church and stared in horror at the scene of utter devastation.

Hundreds of heavy bombers had transformed Caen into a sea of shattered concrete. Walls were still standing, but the bombs had wrought havoc among the blocks of closely packed stone buildings and a mass of rubble stretched as far as the eye could see. Nearly two months after the great bombing attack, bulldozers were still working to clear lanes through the blocked streets, and small groups of silent, haggard civilians wandered through the ruins of what had once been their homes, searching for remnants of their belongings. An appalling stench of death and decay hung over everything.

Hardy summed up the feelings of all three men.

'Jesus,' he muttered, 'this place stinks. Let's get out of it.'

They got back into their jeep. Yeoman settled himself behind the wheel, but before starting up he pulled out his pipe and lit it in the hope that the tobacco smoke would overcome the smell that cloyed his throat.

'It makes you wonder whether all that was really necessary,' Sloane commented as they drove off. 'I thought
we were supposed to liberate the French, not knock hell out of them.'

'Remember that soldier we spoke to earlier—that Pioneer Corps chap?' Hardy interjected. 'He said there weren't any German positions in the town, they were all outside it. Doesn't seem to make sense to me.'

They arrived back at the airfield—their home for three days now—in time for lunch and made for the mess tent, although none of them felt much like eating.

There were no permanent buildings at Carpiquet; all those had been destroyed long since. Everyone now lived under canvas, the crews sleeping in tents pitched close to their aircraft dispersals and snatching hasty meals in a communal mess tent which also served from time to time as a briefing-room. A battered caravan served as an operations-room and had once apparently served for other functions too, because when 380 Squadron took it over it had been knee-deep in empty wine bottles. The airfield's previous occupants had been a wing of Typhoon fighter-bombers; they had left precipitately to another airfield up the coast, hard on the heels of Montgomery's dash towards Belgium.

Yeoman entered the mess tent and stopped in amazement when he saw Yves Romilly sitting disconsolately in a corner, nursing a half-empty glass.

'Yves! What the devil are you doing here? You're supposed to be in Paris for another two days.'

Faithful to his earlier promise, Yeoman had sent Romilly off to the French capital on a short spell of leave as soon as the squadron arrived in France. Something serious must have happened to account for his premature return. The Frenchman looked up at him, and with a shock Yeoman realized that there were tears in his eyes.

'It has changed,' Romilly said softly. 'It has all changed. I never dreamed it would be like it is.'

He took a pack of cigarettes from his pocket, extracted one and lit it. Letting the smoke trickle through his nostrils, he continued:

'I met people I used to call my friends, and they hardly cared to recognize me. They treated me with a kind of contempt, as though blaming me for not having been in Paris through the Occupation. Most of them were wearing

Resistance armbands, although I doubt whether some of them had ever been actively involved.'

Romilly's face was tragic; it was clear that his morale was at a desperately low ebb. Yeoman and the others listened to him in sympathetic silence, knowing that nothing they could say would be of any use.

'They didn't care about us,' Romilly went on. 'They had no time for us, we of the Fighting French, who have striven to uphold the honour of France during four long years of shame. They could speak only of their own experiences under the Germans, of the privations and the danger they had endured.

'Danger!' he said bitterly. His hands were trembling. 'What do they know of danger? They are brave enough now, those scum, shaving the heads of women who slept with the Germans, showing off steel helmets taken from soldiers taken prisoner by someone else!'

Suddenly, he seemed to regain control of himself. Looking hard at Yeoman and the others, he said:

'There will be a reckoning. One day soon, there will be a reckoning.' He threw the butt of his cigarette on the floor and ground it savagely under his heel.

Yeoman sat down, his elbows on the table, and faced the Frenchman.

'Take it easy, Yves,' he said gently. 'We all know how you must feel. Now, why don't you go over to the MO's tent, get yourself a sleeping-pill and turn in for a few hours? You'll feel better for it.'

Romilly shook his head, and Yeoman brought a firmer note into his voice.

'Yves, that's an order.'

Romilly looked at him for a moment, then gave a sigh of resignation.

'*Oui, mon commandant.*' He rose and left the tent.

Tim Sloane stared after him thoughtfully. 'He's cracking up,' he murmured.

'He's had a long war,' Yeoman commented grimly. 'Come to think of it, we've all had a long war. I just hope we can see more of a future at the end of it than Yves can see, right now.'

Privately, he resolved to keep a tactful eye on Yves Romilly; he had a feeling that the Frenchman might be tempted to do something crazy, and he had come too far to throw away his life at this stage in some senseless act of bravado.

During the first week in September 1944, the Allied armies were pushing forward all along the front in hot pursuit of a fleeing enemy. In just four days, the spearheads of Montgomery's British forces covered the astonishing distance of 195 miles, culminating in the capture of Antwerp—its vital port facilities still intact—and the liberation of Brussels amid scenes of wild jubilation. Meanwhile, General Patton's racing US Third Army had reached Verdun, on the Meuse, and General Hodges' US First Army was already probing the defences of the Siegfried Line.

The Battle of France had been won; but everywhere, the Allied armies were meeting stiffening resistance as they approached the frontiers of Germany.

In the air, the Luftwaffe, after its hurried departure from France, had consolidated on airfields east of the Rhine and, thanks to superhuman efforts by the German aircraft industry, had managed to re-equip its front-line squadrons, concentrating on fighters and fighter-bombers at the expense of other types. A few V-I flying-bombs continued to be air-launched against London, but the bulk of these weapons was now directed against objectives in Belgium newly captured by the Allies; hundreds were launched against Antwerp alone.

The people of London had to contend with a new menace. On the evening of 8 September the first V-II rocket impacted in Chiswick. Launched from a mobile base in northern Holland, nearly two hundred miles away, the rocket had arced nearly sixty miles up into space and then plummeted to earth again at a speed of 3,000 mph. Its coming was completely unheralded; there was no warning, as there had been with the v-is. Those in the vicinity of the impact point saw a streak of flame in the sky, like a flash of lightning, as the 46-foot missile—made white hot by friction—plunged down through the last miles of the atmosphere; then came the explosion of its one-ton warhead, followed instantly by the whiplash crack of the supersonic shock wave that chased it down the sky.

The following day the Mosquitos of 380 Squadron were hurriedly despatched to the former Luftwaffe airfield of Le Culot, ten miles south of Louvain in Belgium. The move occurred so quickly that there was no time to send an advance ground party; the ground personnel would have to follow as soon as they could in three-ton trucks.

'Never mind,' a harrassed staff officer at Group HQ told Yeoman over the telephone, 'there are already a couple of Spitfire squadrons at Le Culot; the airfield had been pretty badly knocked about, but it's serviceable all right, Don't worry about a thing, old boy.'

The airfield was indeed badly cratered, but most of the holes had been filled in by troops, willingly assisted by Belgian civilians, and landing presented no problems.

Yeoman went straight to the briefing tent to find out what was going on and found a scene of utter chaos, with RAF types and army liaison officers all apparently getting in each other's way. At length he spotted a wing commander who seemed to be in overall charge and picked his way towards him through the maze of chairs, tables and charts.

'380 Squadron?' the wing commander said, stroking a wispy blond moustache and looking vacantly at Yeoman. 'Sorry, old chap, don't know anything about you.' He stood on tiptoe, peering over the heads of the tent's other occupants, then said: 'Ah, yes. There's the 83 Group liaison type. He might be able to help.'

He pointed to a tall, lean squadron leader who was standing in one corner with a finger stuck in his ear, shouting down a telephone. He had Australia flashes on the shoulders of his battledress blouse and the ribbon of the DFC under his pilot's wings.

Yeoman came to him just as he put the telephone down and stuck out a hand by way of greeting.

'George Yeoman,' he said, '380 Squadron. We've just arrived, and nobody seems to know what to do with us. Any ideas?'

'Bill Forbes,' the other answered. 'Let's see now, 380, 380. Yes. Oh, Christ, yes!' He rummaged in a briefcase and handed Yeoman a bulky folder.

'You were the chaps who bombed the tunnels at St Leu, weren't you? Well take a look at that lot. All German rocket sites around the Hague.'

Yeoman flicked briefly through the folder. It was full of target photographs, maps and various other data on typed sheets of paper.

'Rocket sites?' he queried. 'You don't mean flying-bomb sites? They look pretty similar.'

'No,' said Forbes, 'these are long-range rocket sites. The Huns call the rockets V-IIS and our Intelligence people have known about them for some time. We've photographed them, as you can see. The thing is, we didn't think they'd be operational before we overran that bit of Holland, but we were wrong, because the first one landed in London the day before yesterday, followed in quick succession by several more. We want you to bomb 'em.'

'What,' said Yeoman, appalled, '*all* of them?'

Forbes smiled. 'No, just the ones marked 1 to 6 on the target list. The heavy boys are taking care of the rest. Yours are the most difficult to find.'

'Thanks,' said Yeoman wryly. 'Thanks very much. Can I take all this gen away with me?'

'Sure,' said Forbes readily. 'Just sign here, and take good care of it, Get your boys together and take 'em off to some spare tents you'll find next to where the Spitfire boys are billeted; you can use them for your accommodation and whatever else you need. We're having to rough it at the moment, I'm afraid, until we get properly organized.'

As Yeoman turned to leave, Forbes added: 'Oh, by the way, don't bother dashing around in a mad panic in search of armament officers and so on. Fact is, we haven't got any 500-lb bombs for you yet; they're due to arrive in the morning.'

The tents assigned to 380 Squadron were completely devoid of even the most primitive furniture, and seemed to have been pitched on the muddiest patch of ground on the airfield. Yeoman and his crews surveyed them with dismay.

'Right,' said Yeoman, 'let's get organized. Yves and Tim, you stay here with me; there are things I want to discuss with you. I'm sending the rest of you off on a scrounging expedition. Happy, you're in charge. See if you can find stores, if there are any. We need duckboards, paliasses, blankets—you know the sort of thing. If you can't get them by legal means...' He left the sentence unfinished, but looked at them meaningfully, producing a number of broad grins as they departed on their errand.

Yeoman found a patch of dry gound and sat down with Romilly and Sloane to study the target folder Forbes had given him. They were still studying it two hours later, when the foraging party returned clinging precariously to an army truck that was laden with all the equipment Yeoman had asked for, and more besides. Within minutes the tents had been converted into billets which, if not exactly snug, would at least keep the crews warm and dry—and there was enough gear stowed away for the ground personnel when they eventually arrived.

Last of all, Hardy reverently unloaded a prodigious quantity of wine and beer. Yeoman stared at it in awe.

'Good God, Happy,' he said. 'Where on earth did you find that?'

'Oh, don't worry, skipper,' his redoubtable navigator replied. 'They'll never miss it.'

Who 'they' were, Yeoman never found out; and he never bothered to make enquiries.

On the eastern fringe of the Hague, the Dutch seat of government, lie the Hague Woods, a long expanse of greenery stretching over a mile and a half from south-west to north-east. They are bisected by New East India Lane; beyond this, in the north-eastern half, is a long lake, and adjacent to the lake is an ancient building that is part of Holland's heritage—the 'Huis den Bosch', or House in the Wood. Built in 1645 as a palace for the Consort of the Prince of Orange, the walls of the Huis den Bosch, over the centuries, witnessed many of history's milestones. In 1899 the world's first international peace conference was held there.

That was ironic, for in the autumn of 1944 war arrived on the doorstep of the Huis den Bosch in the form of one of the most futuristic weapons science had devised—the V-II rocket.

The Germans installed a battery of the missiles in a woodland clearing close to the shore of the lake, only a couple of hundred yards from the House. The location was spotted purely by chance by an RAF reconnaissance pilot, who actually saw one of the rockets being launched.

'There was a bright flash on the ground,' he reported, 'and then I saw the V-II emerging from the trees on a long column of flame at what seemed no more than a few miles an hour. It was wobbling slightly at first, then it gathered speed and accelerated at a fantastic rate, straight up in front of my nose, I kept its vapour trail in sight until it disappeared at what must have been more than fifty thousand feet.

Braving intense light flak, the reconnaissance pilot made two low runs over the site and secured the photographs that formed part of the collection in the target folder given to Yeoman. To the RAF Intelligence experts who had studied them earlier, it was immediately apparent that the Germans had selected this site because they believed that the Allied air forces would not dare to attack it for fear of hitting the ancient building. They were wrong.

Fifteen Mosquitos of 380 Squadron, led by Yeoman, attacked on the evening of 10 September. After flying a long curve out of Belgium they came in low from the North

Sea, straight out of the setting sun. Running the gauntlet of the light flak that spewed at them from gun positions along the promenade bordering the beach they thundered across the rooftops of the town, their bomb-doors open.

In pairs, flying almost wing-tip to wing-tip, they roared down the broad ribbon of the Van Alkemadelaan, bringing traffic below to a screeching halt. Dutch civilians danced in the street and waved frantically to them as they streaked overhead in a thunderclap of noise at more than 300 mph.

Ropes of glowing tracer streaked towards them as they sped towards the long lake, shimmering among the trees in the evening sunlight, but the Germans were powerless to disrupt the whirlwind attack now. Yeoman was the first to bomb, closely followed by Pilot Officer Grinton. There was a jolt as the two 500-lb bombs fell away, a brief glimpse of camouflaged objects in the clearing below, and then they were over and away, hurtling past the old house, pulling round in a hard turn back towards the coast.

Yeoman looked back; the other fourteen Mosquitos were still with him, climbing away hard, weaving through the dark spattering of flak bursts.

Behind them, a section of the Hague Woods vanished in the explosions of thirty delayed-action bombs. A great fountain of smoke shot into the sky, towering over the buildings, and a split second later there was a bright flash and an expanding bubble of flame that denoted the explosion of the v-iis' fuel dump.

The great column of smoke was still visible miles out to sea, even when the shoreline had receded. Yeoman called up the other pilots over the R/T and learned that although some of the Mosquitos had been hit by shell splinters or machine-gun bullets, none of them had sustained serious damage. The only human injury was to Romilly's navigator, who had collected a metal sliver in his thigh. It was a jubilant squadron that returned to Le Culot half an hour later.

During the next few days 380 Squadron attacked five more v-ii sites in Holland, with favourable results on each occasion. The last two targets, both near Leiden, were found to be only lightly defended, so after bombing the Mosquitos attacked the objectives with cannon fire. In doing so they sustained the only loss during the series of anti-v-II sorties: Warrant Officer Laurie's Mosquito was hit by flak in the starboard engine, which blew up. Nevertheless, Laurie managed to steer the crippled aircraft back over Allied-occupied territory, where he and his navigator baled out safely.

His squadron's successes had led Yeoman to believe that they would be ordered to carry out more attacks on the v-II sites, but the course of events decreed otherwise.

On the morning of 16 September, all wing and squadron commanders were summoned to a briefing at Tactical Air HQ in Brussels for an urgent briefing. It was delivered by the officer commanding the Second Tactical Air Force, an air vice-marshal, and he got straight to the point. Behind him, as he stood on the dais, was a huge wall map of Holland and Northern Germany, with large circles drawn about several points on the Lower Rhine.

'Tomorrow morning, gentlemen,' the Air Vice-Marshal began, 'we hope that history will be made. In a combined operation code-named "Market Garden", two American airborne divisions will drop on and capture the crossings of the Waal and the Maas at Nijmegen and Grave, and hold the road between Eindhoven and Grave. At the same time'—he pointed to the map—'the British First Airborne Division has the task of seizing the bridge over the Rhine here, at Arnhem.'

A mutter ran round the room and there were a few low, speculative whistles.

The Air Vice-Marshal held up a hand for silence, then went on:

'Once these objectives are secure, the armoured columns of the British Second Army will be in a position to drive up the narrow corridor from Eindhoven in a fast dash to the Rhine and link up with the most northerly of the airborne elements at Arnhem. It will be the largest airborne

130

operation so far attempted, with one thousand troop-carrying aircraft and five hundred gliders involved.'

He paused and surveyed the packed room for several moments. Then he said:

'It is also, we believe, one of the boldest and imaginative schemes so far devised. If it succeeds—and it must succeed—then Field Marshal Montgomery believes that it will be a first step to opening a corridor for an armoured thrust directly across northern Germany to Berlin itself, in the hope of bringing the war to a speedy conclusion.'

'I'm all in favour of that,' Yeoman murmured to the man next to him, the commander of a Typhoon fighter-bomber Wing. 'It seems a hell of a long way to Arnhem from Eindhoven, though.'

'Forty miles,' the other whispered back, 'and that's as the crow flies. Bloody sight longer by road.'

The briefing went on. Other senior officers, group commanders and various specialists, took the Air Vice-Marshal's place, and gradually a complete picture unfolded of the massive air support operation that the units of Second TAF would be required to provide. While squadrons of Spitfires kept the Luftwaffe at bay, the light bomber and fighter-bomber units would attack enemy barracks, communications and known concentrations of troops and armour in the Arnhem area.

Then came the shock. With attitudes ranging from astonishment to frank disbelief, the assembled pilots heard a senior air staff officer tell them that Second TAF would remain clear of the Arnhem sector during the intitial air drop and also during subsequent drops of reinforcements and supplies—for fear that the British aircraft might become disastrously tangled with formations of patrolling American fighters.

The Typhoon Wing Commander voiced the thoughts of most of them as he and Yeoman had a smoke and a cup of tea before returning to their respective units.

'It seems bloody senseless to me,' he said, 'They'll need us most when they're consolidating, just after they've hit the ground. Nobody mentioned anything about smoke markers to indicate enemy positions, and there doesn't seem to be anything like an adequate ground-to-air radio link. And as for getting mixed up with the Americans—Christ, I've never heard such bloody nonsense. And what happens if the weather clamps? Why, our Typhoons fly in weather the Yanks won't even look at, *and* we find our targets too.'

The Wing Commander looked suddenly grave. 'No, old boy,' he said forcefully, 'things don't look promising. That's what you get when you've a big operation planned by a lot of generals sitting on their arses in London, instead of by chaps who are up the sharp end and who know a bit about what goes on. If you ask me, it could turn into an almighty cock-up.'

Even he could have had no idea how disastrously and tragically prophetic his words would turn out to be.

380 Squadron flew its first mission in support of the Arnhem landings at 1045 the next morning, an hour before the paratroops were due to make their drop. Sixteen Mosquitos were airborne, their assigned target an enemy Panzer barracks on the north-east outskirts of the town of Arnhem itself, In four tight boxes of four aircraft, making a diamond-shaped formation, they crossed the Albert Canal and entered Dutch territory, their course taking them over the fringes of the battered town of Eindhoven, in the vicinity of which the RAF had many times attacked power stations and the big Phillips factory, which produced electronic components for the Luftwaffe and the enemy air defence systems. There was a lot of smoke to the south of the town, where a tank battle appeared to be in progress around the village of Valkenswaard; above it, squadrons of Typhoons wheeled like birds of prey, with flights breaking away from time to time to fire their rockets at some unseen target.

Yeoman warned his crews to keep a good lookout—not so much for enemy fighters as for other Allied aircraft, of which the sky was full. It was a bright, sunny Sunday morning, with excellent visibility, and the sight of formations of Spitfires, sweeping the sky ahead, was a comforting one to the Mosquito crews. They would have little to fear from the Luftwaffe; the flak—and there was plenty of it in the Arnhem area—would be their main concern.

'Volkel's taking a pasting,' said Hardy, looking out beyond the Mosquito's starboard wing-tip. Yeoman glanced across: in the distance, over Volkel aerodrome, fighters—impossible to tell whether Spitfires or US Mustangs at this distance—were swarming like hornets, making their strafing runs and then climbing away fast through clusters of anti-aircraft bursts.

'Rather them than us,' Yeoman muttered, recalling his own bitter experiences of attacking enemy airfields.

The Mosquitos sped over another arrow-straight canal, and then a railway-line. On the latter the wreckage of a locomotive, the victim no doubt of the Typhoon's attentions, was smouldering gently. They crossed the broad, shining band of the River Maas at Grave, where the US 101st Airborne Division was scheduled to drop, and then thundered over the Waal north-west of Nijmegen, the objective of the US 82nd Airborne.

They turned north along a railway-line that joined another at right-angles between Arnhem and the village of Oosterbeek. Beyond the junction, on the edge of a wood, was the Panzer barracks that was their target.

'Christ,' exclaimed Hardy as they drew nearer. 'Look at that, will you?'

Yeoman saw at once what the navigator meant. The sky over and around Arnhem was black with aircraft. A squadron of Mosquitos in ragged formation, one of them trailing smoke from an engine, slid past a few hundred yards to port, heading in the opposite direction, and a few moments later three flights of American Thunderbolt fighters cut across 380 Squadron's noses and turned in from the beam, checking the Mosquitos' identities before sweeping off to the south.

From the corner of the woods beyond the railway

junction, columns of smoke were rising. Above them, more Mosquitos were twisting and turning through a maze of anti-aircraft fire.

'It looks like some bastard has pinched our target,' Yeoman said over the intercom. Then, to the rest of the Squadron, he ordered: 'Straight in and straight out, chaps. No heroics. Bomb on my signal.'

He had seldom seen such flak. It came at them from all sides and the sky all around was filled with flashes and explosions. The pilots needed all their willpower to hold a steady course.

The enemy barracks, a cluster of sheds and low buildings surrounded by pine trees and partly obscured by smoke from the previous attack, was coming up under the nose. The formation headed for it in a shallow dive. Yeoman took the middle of a group of large sheds as his aiming point and forced himself to keep a steady voice as he issued his instructions over the R/T. The sky was filled with blinding, multi-coloured light and the smoke of the shell bursts streamed past the aircraft as they swept down towards the target. Shell splinters rattled on wings and fuselage.

'Bombing... bombing... now!'

The sixteen pilots pressed their bomb releases simultaneously on Yeoman's signal and thirty-two 500-lb bombs curved away as the Mosquitos came out of their dive. The formation now broke up and scattered on Yeoman's command, each aircraft weaving crazily away from the nightmare cauldron of fire.

Over the radio, a voice said quietly: 'Blue Four. I'm hit. Trying to—' Flight Sergeant Parker's words were cut off in mid-sentence.

Pulling his aircraft round in a tight turn, Yeoman saw a Mosquito plunging vertically to earth, racked by glaring explosions as its fuel tanks went up in flames. It hit the ground in a rippling bubble of fire, scattering fragments over a wide area.

The target area was completely covered by a great pall of

dust and smoke. Yeoman had no intention of making a run over the top to try and observe results. He pressed the R/T button.

'Come on, let's get out of here. Form up on me.'

One by one, to the south of Arnhem, the Mosquitos came swinging in to rejoin the formation. On the way back, a few miles east of S'Hertogenbosch, they dived down to make a vengeful, murderous attack on an enemy motorized column, raking it with cannon fire until their ammunition was expended. When they had finished, the road was littered with shattered and burning vehicles along a two-mile stretch.

Forty minutes later, as the nerve-taut men of the Allied fighter squadrons tore hungrily into a hasty meal and awaited further orders, the first waves of the gigantic armada of transport aircraft and gliders thundered over the flat Dutch landscape en route for their objectives.

In the towns and villages around the dropping zones, the people of Holland, emerging from church in their Sunday best, gazed up in speechless awe as the vanguard of the great five hundred mile long sky train roared overhead, disgorging thousands of coloured parachutes, unaware of the desperate battles that were soon to engulf them and their neat little homes.

# Chapter Eleven

From fifteen thousand feet, Yeoman and Hardy looked down on the flames of Arnhem: a glowing, flickering eye, dull red and evil in the surrounding darkness.

'Poor devils,' Yeoman said quietly. There was nothing else to say; no other words to describe the misery and horror that was the fate of the decimated remnants of the First British Airborne Division.

For a week they had held on gallantly, in the face of terrible odds. Before the drop, the paratrooper commanders had been told that they would have little to fear; that the Germans in the Arnhem area were in disarray and were beginning to recruit invalids, boys and old men. Instead, they had encountered battle-hardened troops of the élite Waffen ss, German paratroops and two Panzer divisions which, according to Intelligence, had not existed. Moreover, the German forces were led by able and experienced generals such as Kurt Student, whose airborne forces had captured Crete in 1941 and been on the brink of invading Malta the following year.

The air drop had gone wrong from the very beginning. Since not enough transport aircraft had been available to carry the whole of the Airborne Division, much had depended on a vital reinforcement drop the following day, 18 September, but this had been delayed by bad weather. Meanwhile, although part of the first wave of paratroops had captured the vital bridge and held on to it, fierce counterattacks soon split the airborne force into three separate pockets.

The Americans at Grave and Nijmegen had fared much

better, but the armoured spearheads of the British 30th Corps, advancing up the narrow corridor from Eindhoven, had met much stiffer resistance than they had anticipated, with consequent delays to their timetable. In particular, they had found that the approaches to the bridge at Nijmegen were heavily defended, and it was some time before they had been able to hammer their way through to link up with the American airborne troops.

Even after that, the nature of the countryside—a maze of dykes and ditches—meant that the British tanks had been forced to keep to the long, narrow road that ran from Nijmegen to Arnhem, and the armoured column had to fight for every yard of the ten-mile journey. By that time, the battle for Arnhem was already lost. The remnants of the Airborne Division, utterly exhausted, devoid of food, water and ammunition despite the heroic efforts of the Allied air transport squadrons—who braved murderous anti-aircraft fire and took appalling losses only to release their cargoes over dropping zones which were now in enemy hands—were gradually being forced to surrender.

Apart from the attack on the Panzer barracks just before the airborne assault, 380 Squadron had played no direct part in support of the Arnhem operation. Together with the other Mosquito FB V-I squadrons of Second Tactical Air Force, it had been employed exclusively on night intruder sorties, the Mosquitos striking singly at airfields deep inside Germany.

The task of maintaining air cover over the First Airborne Division had fallen to the Spitfire squadrons, but their operations had been continually hampered by bad weather. Day after day the rainclouds had been stacked up in heavy layers, and in the frequent torrential downpours the fighter pilots had been forced to concentrate more on keeping their squadron formations than on keeping a lookout for the enemy. Fortunately, the weather had presented the Luftwaffe with similar problems.

So Yeoman and his pilots had seen little of the air drama unfolding over Arnhem, but they had gleaned a little of it from the harrowing stories told by the crews of a couple of flak-damaged Dakota transports which had made emergency landings at Le Culot. Yeoman would never forget the sight of one of the pilots as the latter huddled by the stove in 380 Squadron's crew tent, white-faced and trembling, clutching a mug of tea and telling his story in staccato sentences:

'I've done three supply drops over Arnhem. I don't want to do a fourth. We've lost half the squadron. The last trip was an absolute bastard...we were supposed to make a formation drop, but it didn't work out that way...got split up in a cloud on the way in. My navigator was right on the ball and we dropped out of the muck right over Arnhem... Jesus, the flak! You could have got out and walked on it.

'There was a Stirling in front of us, dropping its load. It was already on fire. Then it took a direct hit and broke clean in half, just aft of the wing. The front part went down in a great, slow, ponderous spin and blew up on the edge of the town. I could see more aircraft, burning on the ground.

'I just pointed the Dak's nose at where the dropping zone was supposed to be and started praying. I don't mind telling you, I made most of the run with my eyes shut. God only knows how we got through.'

And the Typhoon fighter-bombers of Second TAF, Yeoman thought bitterly, which might have been working wonders in suppressing the enemy flak batteries with their rockets and cannon while the supply drops were taking place, were instead operating a long way to the south, shooting up trains and convoys....

'Steer zero-seven-five, skipper,' Hardy said, breaking into the pilot's thoughts. Yeoman swung the Mosquito round on to the new heading and the red glow that was Arnhem gradually receded into the distance.

Their principal target that night was Rheine, where there was known to be a concentration of night fighters. At least some of the latter were likely to be airborne, for RAF Bomber Command was shortly due to attack the Dortmund–Ems Canal. Yeoman planned to hang around in

138

the vicinity of Rheine for as long as his fuel allowed in the hope of catching some of the enemy aircraft on take-off or landing.

They were still half-way to Rheine when Hardy suddenly picked up a contact on his A-I radar. The blip was still a long way out on the starboard beam, some thousands of feet lower down, and the navigator gave Yeoman a course to steer that should have enabled him to turn right in front of the target and cut it off—the most favourable interception pattern of all.

Hardy called out the range at regular intervals. Suddenly, he swore and ordered:

'Turn left twenty degrees.'

Yeoman pulled the Mosquito round and levelled the wings again. 'What happened?' he asked.

'The bastard went straight across our nose,' Hardy told him. 'I misjudged his speed. He must be going like a blue-arsed fly.'

'Where is he now?'

'Dead ahead, two miles and about two thousand feet lower down.'

Yeoman put down the Mosquito's nose and opened the throttles. The engines howled and the aircraft began to shudder as the speed built up. It made no difference; the blip remained obstinately in the middle of the trace at a range of two miles. Hardy felt an irrational hatred growing inside him as he stared at the tiny, glowing spot of light; it was as though it were mocking him.

The buffeting was getting worse. The controls were stiffened by the speed and the Mosquito was beginning to 'porpoise' slightly, as though riding over a series of waves. Yeoman felt a growing fear that the whole airframe was about to come apart; the engine temperatures were already in the red.

'Still two miles,' Hardy said, 'and still dead ahead.'

Yeoman began to level out cautiously, struggling to control the shuddering aircraft, at the same time peering ahead into the night. After a few moments, he said calmly:

'I think I've got a visual. Twelve o'clock, level. See what you make of it, Happy. But be quick: I can't hold this speed for much longer.

Hardy raised his eyes from his radar display and peered through the windscreen, but could see nothing; the fluorescent images of the cathode ray tube had ruined his night vision for the time being.

'Sorry, skipper,' he muttered, 'can't see a thing. What's it look like?'

'Two red points of light, like stars, very close together. Oh, they're fading now. He's drawing away, going down I think.'

Hardy took another look at his radar; the luminous blip sank slowly and slid off the display. 'That was him all right,' the navigator said. 'I wonder what it was?'

Yeoman throttled back, testing the controls carefully and keeping an anxious eye on the engine instruments as the speed dropped away.

'Definitely a jet job, I should say,' he said. 'Probably one of the new Messerschmitt 262s we've been hearing about. Anyway, we hadn't a hope in hell of catching him.'

Yeoman resumed their heading for Rheine, glancing at the luminous dial of his wristwatch. 'Oh-one-thirty,' he said, as though talking to himself. 'The bombers should be on their way home now. We might just catch the Huns with their pants down, with a bit of luck.'

Luck indeed seemed to be on their side when, a few minutes later, a cluster of twinkling lights appeared on the horizon; the runways at Rheine were brightly lit to recieve the returning night fighters. Some of the latter were already over the airfield, for as they drew nearer Yeoman and Hardy saw multi-coloured recognition flares float down through the night.

Yeoman pushed down the nose and took the Mosquito in a dive to less than a thousand feet, the height at which an aircraft normally flew around an aerodrome circuit. By keeping below it, he hoped to be able to spot the enemy fighters silhouetted against the night sky.

The lit-up main runway was approaching fast now and Yeoman crossed the end of it at right-angles before turning on to the downwind leg of the circuit. The engine exhausts crackled and popped as he throttled back, lowering the undercarriage and a few degrees of flap and reducing to circuit speed so as not to overshoot anything ahead of him.

Hardy already had a radar contact ahead and above and was rapidly counting off the dwindling range. Yeoman looked up, saw almost immediately that it was very close, and identified it without difficulty as a Junkers 88 night fighter. Its wheels were down and he could clearly see the array of radar antennae festooned around its nose.

It was too close for comfort, so he reduced the speed still further and dropped back a little, keeping the Junkers in sight all the time. Then, opening the throttles again, he pulled up behind the enemy aircraft and opened fire almost at point-blank range into the long, black fuselage.

Vivid flames streamed back and Yeoman pulled sharply off to one side, raising his own undercarriage and flaps as he did so. There was no need for a second attack; the Junkers was finished. The burning mass went down in a steep dive and exploded beside the runway in a cascade of blazing wreckage.

The runway lights went out abruptly. At low level, Yeoman took the Mosquito away from the airfield and cruised around for several minutes.

'Might as well let the fuss die down,' he said. 'They'll put the lights on again shortly; the Huns in the circuit are bound to be low on fuel.'

After ten minutes he turned and edged back towards Rheine, still keeping low, while Hardy searched for more contacts among the echoes from the ground that cluttered his radar screen.

Suddenly, the runway lights came on again.

'Have you found anything yet, Happy?' Yeoman asked. Hardy was glued to his radar set.

'I'm not sure,' the navigator said. 'There seems to be something, but it's very faint…hard to distinguish among the ground clutter. Seems to be on the same level as us, or perhaps a little below...coming in to land, maybe.'

Yeoman stared hard at the runway approach lights, which were coming towards them at an angle of forty-five degrees. They seemed to flicker slightly, as though a shadow was fleeting over them.

With a start, Yeoman realized that he was seeing the silhouette of an aircraft, its dark shape obscuring the lights for a fraction of a second as it flew over them towards the end of the runway. He turned in after it, trying to work out where it would touch down, knowing that as soon as it landed the runway lights would probably be extinguished and that he would lose his target in the shadows.

'Careful, skipper,' warned Hardy. 'It might be another Mossie, up to the same thing as us.'

'Don't think so,' the pilot muttered. 'He's landing all right, reducing speed now as he crosses the threshold. There he goes, touching down now; I can just see him. Damn!'

Yeoman's exclamation was caused by the sudden extinction of the runway lights. In that same split second, his thumb jabbed down on the firing-button. Four glowing lines of cannon shells burst from the Mosquito's nose, exploding on the concrete of the runway and the dark shape that had just settled on it.

The Mosquito swept over the top of the target with only feet to spare and Yeoman pulled the stick into his right thigh, opening the throttles and taking the aircraft into a steep climbing turn. A bright orange flash from somewhere behind him lit the interior of the cockpit briefly, then died away to a fading glow as they sped away.

'Did you see what it was, Happy?' the pilot asked.

'No, I didn't,' Hardy replied. 'But I think it was twin-engined. It certainly went off with a hell of a bang.'

'Good enough,' Yeoman said. 'It's time we went home. We've got just about enough fuel to make it. We seem to have stirred up a proper wasps' nest back there.'

Behind them, the sky over Rheine was a spectacular

display of anti-aircraft fire. After a while it died away as the enemy gunners realized that there was nothing to shoot at. Yeoman set course for home, juggling with the throttles and the fuel mixture as he gained altitude to give them a few extra minutes' flying time.

The flight back to Le Culot was uneventful. Yeoman found that he was the last to land; the other Mosquitos which had been out on the night's operations had returned some minutes earlier, and the crews were debriefing.

It had been a successful night for the squadron, as Freddie Barnes lost no time in telling Yeoman. The Intelligence Officer's face lit up as the squadron commander came into the briefing tent.

'That's everyone back safely,' he said, 'and with your two Huns the night's score is six. Considering the weather conditions, that's pretty good.'

Yeoman smiled at Barnes's understatement and gratefully sipped the mug of scalding tea someone handed to him. Looking round, he caught Tim Sloane's eye and waved him over. Sloane's promotion to squadron leader had just come through; on the epaulettes of his battledress, he had pushed his flight lieutenant's bars apart to make room for the new, shiny strip of blue braid.

'Well, Tim,' Yeoman said, 'it's all yours. I'm pleased that you've got the squadron.'

'Thanks for recommending me,' Sloane answered. 'When are you leaving?'

'Tomorrow afternoon. No time for a farewell party, I'm afraid. I'll be on the duty Anson and out of this place like a shot!'

'We'll be around to see you off,' Sloane assured him. He hesitated for a moment, then said:

'I hope I can do as good a job as you've done, George. I've a lot to live up to. It's been good working with you.'

They left the tent. Outside, Yeoman shook hands with Hardy.

'Thanks for all your efforts, Happy. We've been a good

team. Well, that's it; we've flown our last operation with 380 Squadron.'

But he was wrong.

# Chapter Twelve

It was pouring with rain, and although he had covered the few yards from his tent to the operations caravan at a run Yeoman was already soaking wet. Dragged from a deep sleep by the urgent summons of the orderly officer, he had pulled on a greatcoat over his pyjamas and thrust his bare feet into his flying boots.

Panting slightly, he picked up the telephone, The senior air staff officer of 83 Group was on the line.

'Yeoman, I'd like you to come up to Air HQ right away. We've a very urgent job for you and your squadron to do. Very urgent indeed.'

Taking a deep breath, Yeoman said: 'Sir, I'm due to leave this afternoon. Squadron Leader Sloane has assumed command.'

'I realize that, Yeoman,' the Group Captain replied, 'but we need your experience for this job. Your tour is up and we can't order you to do it, of course. We're asking you to volunteer.'

All Yeoman's instincts warned him to say no, that he'd had enough, that all he wanted to do was crawl back into bed and sleep through the rest of the morning. Instead, he said: 'All right, sir. I'll be there as soon as I can.'

'Good man. I knew we could depend on you.'

Yeoman was at Air HQ in Brussels ninety minutes later, after a hair-raising drive along sodden, pitted roads that were congested with long convoys of armour and trucks, all heading towards the front. On arrival, he was immediately shown into a room where the Group Captain was waiting for him, together with 83 Group's Senior

Intelligence Officer, a Wing Commander.

The Group Captain came straight to the point.

'Yeoman, take a look at the map. You see this place here?'

Yeoman leaned over the table and saw that the Group Captain was pointing to a small village some forty miles inside Germany; its name was Berge and it lay in heavily wooded country. With his professional eye, Yeoman also noted that it lay in a triangle formed by the three enemy fighter airfields of Rheine, Ahlhorn and Steinfeld.

'Yes, sir, I see it. It doesn't look very impressive.'

'It wasn't,' said the Intelligence Officer, 'until a couple of weeks ago, when it suddenly became stiff with ss troops and ringed with anti-aircraft guns. You can see their positions on these photographs, here.'

The Wing Commander produced a series of air reconnaissance shots of the village, taken both vertically and obliquely. Arrows pointed to the flak batteries.

'What we are interested in,' the Wing Commander continued, 'is this building here.' He pointed to a large house situated close to the north-east corner of the village; it lay in a park, bordered by woodland.

'Briefly, Yeoman,' the Group Captain broke in, 'we want that house destroyed. More specifically, we want the people in it killed. We can't achieve that by means of a medium-level attack, because it would give them plenty of warning to evacuate. It's got to be a low-level affair, achieving complete surprise—the kind of thing your squadron has carried out several times over the past year with considerable success, if I may say so.'

'Thank you, sir,' Yeoman said, pleased by the compliment. 'May I ask who our intended victims are?'

The Group Captain shook his head. 'Even I don't know that, Yeoman. All I know is that the building appears to be an important headquarters of the Abwehr, the German equivalent of MI5, and that we've had top priority orders from London to destroy it and whoever is in there. How soon can you do it? Time, we are told, is vitally important.'

'As soon as the weather lifts,' Yeoman answered, 'if I can get back to Le Culot straight away and begin the planning.' He looked at the Wing Commander. 'Is there any more Intelligence on what sort of opposition we're likely to expect?'

'No. It's all there, in the target folder. The flak will be your main problem. With luck, you can be in and out before the fighters from Rheine and so on have time to react.'

'Let's hope so,' Yeoman said. 'The boys aren't going to like this, though; the squadron was supposed to be stood down for a couple of days after last night's show.'

'Yeoman,' said the Group Captain quietly, 'if you pull this one off, I'll stand the squadron down for a week, and you can tell them so. Now, good luck to you.'

Yeoman shook hands with both the senior officers, saluted, and went out into the driving rain.

Yeoman looked around the faces of the crews assembled in the briefing tent, Including himself and Hardy, twenty men were present; he had calculated that ten Mosquitos, each armed with two 500-lb bombs, would be more than adequate to carry out the attack.

All the men looked tired and drawn, and with good reason. Yves Romilly was showing more signs of strain than ever; he had developed a fierce twitch in his left cheek. Romilly, Yeoman decided, would have to come off operations. He would have a word with Tim Sloane about that.

'All right,' Yeoman said. 'Synchronize your watches. It is now 1600 minus ten seconds...five...four...three...two...one...now! Let's get on with it.'

They went out to their Mosquitos, Overhead the sky was still leaden, but the cloud base had gone up to three thousand feet. Yeoman was glad of the clouds; they would provide excellent cover if enemy fighters appeared.

The Mosquitos took off and formed up over the airfield. Then, as though held together by invisible threads, they set course together on a heading of 035 degrees. They thundered into Holland, flying over the flat, waterlogged Dutch landscape at five hundred feet, heading for the town of Zwolle at the end of the first 125-mile leg of their flight; they would then turn due east towards their objective. The dog-leg course would serve two purposes. First, it would lead the enemy to believe that they were heading for a target in the extreme north of Germany, or perhaps in Denmark; and it would take them well to the north of Rheine, the scene of Yeoman's visit the previous night.

Some flak came up at them as they entered enemy territory beyond Nijmegen, but it was sporadic and did no harm. The roads here seemed almost deserted, in contrast to the constant flow of movement on the Allied side of the front line; it was a silent testimony to the complete air superiority which had been achieved by the Second TAF. Such was the fear of the marauding Typhoons that the enemy convoys now dared move only by night.

Mixed feelings surged through Yeoman as he glanced at the other Mosquitos, flying compactly on either side of him and behind; feelings of anticipation at the coming action, mingled with nostalgia and regret. This was—must be—the very last time that he would ever lead the Mosquito Squadron into action. It would have been better, in a way, if he had ended it all as planned with last night's intruder sortie, and then slipped quietly away. He hated farewells, and was glad that his closest friend on the squadron, Happy Hardy, was leaving with him. Their departure would have to be put off until tomorrow, now.

The minutes ticked by. The ten Mosquitos drummed low over the rooftops of Apeldoorn and the crews caught brief glimpses of people waving frantically to them from the streets below. Someone fired a machine-gun at them from what appeared to be a group of enemy armoured cars in a square, but the tracer fell harmlessly behind the speeding formation. A few moments later the town receded astern.

'Turning-point coming up in five minutes, skipper,'

Hardy announced in his laconic fashion.

They crossed the straight band of the Apeldoorn Canal. Beyond it wound the River Ijssel, flanked by a railway line on either side. As usual Hardy had hit their turning-point right on the nose.

'Stand by to turn in ten seconds,' the navigator said. 'Zero-nine-five degrees. Turn...turn...now!'

Followed by the rest of the formation, Yeoman brought his Mosquito sweeping round towards the east, settling down on the new heading. Five minutes later they were entering Germany, flying over marshy moorland.

A few miles to the south was Twenthe airfield, one of the three attacked by 380 Squadron on their very first operational mission more than a year ago. Yeoman himself had attacked Twenthe, together with Terry Saint and two NCOS, Flight Sergeant Miller and Sergeant Telfer. Of those four crews, only he and Hardy were now left; and of the original complement of 380 Squadron, only Romilly, Sloane and Lorrimer now remained except for themselves. The others were all replacements.

They flew on over a barren landscape; there was not much habitation in this part of north-west Germany, which was just as well for them, for habitation—especially where it was linked with industry—meant flak.

It began to rain again. Hardy switched on the windscreen wipers and their steady beat sent the water streaming in rivulets along the sides of the cockpit canopy. Peering ahead through the windscreen, Yeoman asked:

'What's that river up ahead, Happy?'

'It's the Ems. We'll cross it about a mile south of a little hamlet called Dalum, and the target is exactly eighteen miles further on. I hope this weather doesn't get any worse, though. Visibility's down to about four miles already.'

The navigator was right; a rainy mist was creeping over the forest that lay beyond the Ems. It would be touch and go whether they would reach the objective in time to make an accurate attack; the light was already beginning to fail and the cloud base seemed to be lowering.

149

They roared across the river and drove on down a broad valley, flanked by masses of tall pines. For the first time, Yeoman broke radio silence.

'Target ahead in four minutes. Attack formation. Watch out for high ground on either side of Berge.'

The village was flanked by two large hills which had given it its name. The largest was 330 feet above sea level at its peak, rising above the tree-tops of the surrounding forest.

To achieve maximum effect and accuracy Yeoman planned to attack in line astern, the Mosquitos plunging singly through the gap between the hills which, fortuitously, acted as a kind of built-in pointer to the location of the big house that was their target. The attack plan called for the pilots to drop their bombs from low level on to a concrete driveway that led up to the main door of the building; the bombs would then bounce through a short trajectory and impact on the walls of the house, it was hoped, with devastating effect. The 'skip-bombing' technique was not new; it had already been used with success in missions against small targets by other Mosquito squadrons of Second TAF, and by the Americans in anti-shipping attacks in the Pacific.

Yeoman hoped that the first three or four Mosquitos, with himself in the lead, might be able to get through the gap and make their bomb runs before the flak gunners realized what was happening. They could then turn and silence at least some of the flak with their 20-mm cannon while the remainder of the squadron made their attacks. Each Mosquito would attack at a twelve-second interval behind the one ahead to avoid the explosions of the bombs, which were fitted with eight-second delayed-action fuses.

The next few minutes would tell whether the plan was going to work.

Yeoman took the Mosquito down to within a few feet of the valley floor and opened the throttles.

'Here goes, Happy. Bomb-doors open.'

The navigator reached forward and pulled the bomb-doors selector. There was the usual slight buffeting sensation as the doors came down, accompanied by a nose-up change in the trim of the aircraft, which the pilot quickly corrected.

The Mosquito's starboard wing-tip was almost brushing a line of pine trees. Hardy tensed involuntarily as they blurred past. This was the worst time for a navigator, who now had nothing to do but sit there and take whatever was coming to him.

The gap between the two hills leaped towards them. Yeoman could already see the roofs of the village beyond; a moment later he saw the target, the big house situated on a slight rise at the fringe of the woods, just as it had appeared in the photographs. He gave a touch of left rudder, lining up the aircraft carefully as the distance narrowed.

They were through the gap. As always, in these last few instants of a low-level attack, time seemed frozen. Small details, seen with remarkable clarity, impressed themselves indelibly on Yeoman's brain. A squad of soldiers, marching up a village street, scattering as though in slow motion; a four-barrelled anti-aircraft gun, mounted on a tower, swinging round to track the hurtling Mosquito; the massive doors of the big house, flanked by french windows.

He was barely conscious of pressing the bomb-release button. Then, as he pulled back the stick and took the Mosquito plunging over the roof of the house, a sudden violent jolt brought his mind back into proper focus again.

'Christ, skipper,' Hardy yelled, 'that was close! You hit some sort of aerial—I think we've lost a bit of the starboard wing-tip!'

Yeoman pulled the Mosquito round in a tight turn over the tree-tops, flying a curve around the village.

'She's responding okay,' he told the alarmed navigator. 'Look out for the flak posts, Happy.'

He glanced back towards the house in time to see the double explosion of the bombs. Smoke, dust and chunks of flying masonry burst from the far end of the front wall.

'Missed the front door, damn it,' the pilot muttered. Out of the corner of his eye he saw Warrant Officer Laurie's Mosquito beginning its run, holding a dead straight course through a web of 20-mm flak shells which were now rising from all sides.

There was no time to observe Laurie's progress any further, because Yeoman's attention was now occupied with a flak post on a small knoll by the edge of the woods. Diving down, he gave it a burst from his cannon and saw his shells explode among the gun crew, who collapsed like rag dolls.

'Laurie's through all right,' Hardy shouted. 'He hit it right on the nose!'

Yeoman, turning in search of another target, suddenly broke hard right to avoid the third attacking Mosquito, flown by Pilot Officer Grinton. In the fraction of a second it remained in view, he saw a flak shell carry away its complete port wing outboard of the engine. Hardy, looking back, saw Grinton and his navigator die as the remains of their Mosquito veered to one side and crashed into a row of houses, disintegrating in a pillar of flame. A few moments later Pilot Officer Wallace, the fourth pilot in Yeoman's section and a close friend of Grinton's sped through the smoke of the latter's funeral pyre; he released his bombs and jinked away over the trees, turning to join Yeoman and Laurie in their attacks on the gun positions.

The corridor between the dark canopy of the pine forest and the lowering clouds was growing narrower with every passing minute, and was ablaze with glaring light as the four-barrelled 'Vierling' 20-mm flak guns threw their deadly umbrella over the village.

Yves Romilly, leading the second section of Mosquitos, came through the storm and dropped his bombs on target despite being thrown temporarily off course by a shell that punched a big hole in his rudder. The Mosquito behind him, flown by Pilot Officer Crombie, was not so lucky; with both engines streaming flame, it rolled uncontrollably to the left and crashed in the forest, where it was obliterated by the explosion of its own bombs. Crombie's sacrifice, however, probably saved Flight Sergeant Martinsen; the flak gunners, concentrating on Crombie's flaming aircraft, completely ignored the Norwegian and he made his run unmolested, bouncing his bombs squarely into the pulverized ruin of the house.

Five Mosquitos were now hammering at the flak batteries, working their way steadily in towards the village from the outer perimeter of gun posts and drawing fire away from the last section of Mosquitos, led by Tim Sloane. Both he and Flight Sergeant Lorrimer successfully ran the gauntlet and unloaded their bombs into the pall of smoke that now completely obscured the target, but Sergeant Hudson, bringing up the rear, never even reached the village.

No one ever knew what happened. As it sped through the gap between the hills on the final run towards the target, Hudson's Mosquito suddenly hit the ground and bounced high into the air. Yves Romilly, who saw it all, said later that it seemed as though Hudson was trying to regain control and make a forced landing, but the Mosquito ploughed into a line of trees and exploded.

Yeoman used up the last of his cannon shells and turned steeply, his wing-tip almost brushing the tops of the pine trees, to make a low run over the target. Through the drifting smoke he saw that the house was a crumbled ruin, collapsed on itself. He was certain that nothing inside could have survived.

He called up the other pilots and told them to climb up through the cloud, making rendezvous on top of it. They would fly back to Le Culot on a direct course, staying above cloud all the way and diving back into its shelter if they were attacked. It was all they could do, for most of the Mosquitos were out of ammunition.

They broke out of the cloud at eight thousand feet, the Mosquitos popping up one by one into the blinding glare of the setting sun. In formation once more, they flew low over the fleecy white peaks and valleys, like a school of flying fish skimming from wavecrest to wavecrest.

Somewhere in the vicinity of Eindhoven, Yeoman called up base and learned that the cloud base was two thousand feet, giving them plenty of room for manoeuvre after descending through the murk. A 'fix' passed to them by Flying Control confirmed that they were right on course.

Yeoman's thumb hovered over the R/T button, ready to tell his pilots to begin their descent through the cloud and to spread out to reduce the risk of collision, but the words never came.

At that moment, the fighters hit them.

The first indication Yeoman had of impending danger came when the fuel tanks of Arthur Laurie's Mosquito, a hundred yards away on the right, exploded in a splash of orange flame. An instant later, his own aircraft shook with a terrific concussion as something exploded on the starboard side of the fuselage. Splinters rattled against the armour plating of his seat, like stones on a tin roof.

Frantically, he pulled the Mosquito round in the direction of the threat, just in time to see the three fighters before they plunged down into the cloud layer. There was just time, too, to see that they bore the black-and-white stripes of the Allied Expeditionary Air Force.

They were American P-51 Mustangs....

They had mistaken the Mosquitos for Messerschmitt 410s. It was the only possible explanation. Yet the attack had been inexcusable—as inexcusable as Yeoman's own failure to keep a proper lookout.

There was no time for self-recrimination now. Without further delay, he led the surviving Mosquitos down through the cloud, following the heading given to him by Hardy.

The navigator was white-faced and shaking. Yeoman looked at him anxiously and asked if he was all right.

Hardy smiled weakly. 'Fine, skipper. Just fine. A bit shaken, that's all. Just stop wandering off course, will you?'

It was the first time Yeoman had ever seen Hardy smile.

The six Mosquitos landed at Le Culot a few minutes

later, in driving rain. Yeoman taxied to his dispersal and shut down the engines. He glanced over at the now silent Hardy, who was staring out of the side window of the cockpit.

'Come on, Happy,' the pilot said. 'Open the hatch, will you? Let's get some fresh air.'

There was no answer. Yeoman reached out and shook the navigator by the shoulder, Hardy's head rolled round towards him.

'Oh, no,' Yeoman said. 'Oh, Jesus, no!'

The navigator's eyes were wide open, but there was no light in them. And it was only then that Yeoman saw the rent in Hardy's flying jacket, and the congealed blood.

# Epilogue

Yeoman sat in the darkness, staring disconsolately through the window of the little apartment in Earl's Court into the greater darkness of wartime London, noting abstractly that the blackout was not as perfect as it might have been, for here and there a glimmer of light shone.

His fingers played with the key Julia had given him at their last meeting, and he wondered yet again what could have happened to her. The apartment had been cold and miserable, as though no one had lived in it for weeks; that in itself was not strange, because he knew that Julia's work as a correspondent often entailed lengthy absences.

But this was 7 October, her birthday and the day they had arranged to meet, come hell or high water. As time went by he became more and more anxious, more apprehensive that something bad might have happened to her.

There had been no message in the apartment; nothing to explain her absence. None of the neighbours had seen her for some time.

He stared at the telephone, willing it to ring. It remained obstinately silent.

After a while, he told himself that he was being a fool, that soon she would come in through the door, or at least give him a call. He got up, drew the curtains and lit the fire, for the October evening was chilly. Then he made himself a cup of tea and resumed his lonely vigil.

Two miles across London from the apartment, three men sat in a shabby, sparsely furnished room in Whitehall and listened to the sonorous boom of Big Ben. Automatically, they looked at their watches; it was 2000.

Air Commodore Sampson was the first to speak. 'In God's name,' he said quietly, 'why 380 Squadron? And why Yeoman?'

The man who answered him was silver-haired, with a fierce moustache. He spoke in clipped, precise tones.

'Because we knew they could do the job better than anyone else, with his leadership. We had to be certain, you see, of utterly destroying the house and the people in it. I'm sorry about the losses the squadron suffered; I know that you hold it, and Yeoman, in high esteem. But the job had to be done.'

'It just doesn't seem right, somehow,' Sampson muttered, 'sending those chaps out to kill our own people. Especially in view of Yeoman's involvement—' He left the sentence unfinished, waving his hand instead over an open folder that lay on the table in front of him. It contained a photograph and some typewritten sheets of paper.

'It was necessary,' the silver-haired man said firmly. 'Sooner or later, those SOE agents held captive in that house would have talked. We couldn't take the risk.'

The third man in the room spoke suddenly, in the soft drawl of the American south.

'I think we owe the Air Commodore a little more explanation than that, Bernard,' he said. 'Perhaps I'm laying my neck on the line by saying anything at all, but here goes anyway.'

He looked hard at Sampson for a moment, then said:

'The SOE operatives in question had been involved for some time in establishing contact with a small group of German scientists engaged in secret weapons research, Air Commodore. They were bitterly disillusioned with the Nazis, and as long ago as the autumn of 1943 had become convinced that Germany *must* lose the war, for humanity's sake.'

He leaned forward slightly in his chair, 'They had already smuggled certain vital information out to us concerning new jet- and rocket-powered weapons,' he continued. 'Then, a few months ago, we got a hint of something really big, a weapon so devastating that it will make the biggest bombs we've got seem like firecrackers. Air Commodore, have you ever heard of an atomic bomb?'

'Well, I know the theory, of course,' Sampson replied, 'but I don't see—'

'The Germans are working hard to build one,' the American interrupted.

'The scientists I'm talking about are involved in the project. That's why we've got to win the war soon, Sampson. Can you imagine the possible consequences if we don't?'

The Air Commodore nodded soberly.

'Well,' the American continued, 'our German scientists realize the consequences too, and that's why they decided to help us. We set up an SOE escape line for them, Sampson, but something went badly wrong and, as you know, some of our top operatives were captured.'

He tightened his lips and drummed his fingertips on the table.

'We had to kill them, Sampson. There was no alternative. You know the Germans' interrogation methods. If they had learned the identities of the scientists who are helping us they would have executed them immediately— and we need those men. We need them because we must know about the German atomic project, and because their knowledge will be vital to us in other ways. Somehow, we'll get them out.'

'I see,' the Air Commodore said slowly. 'But... how can you be sure that your operatives hadn't talked already—or that they were killed in the attack?'

'They didn't talk,' the American said. 'We'd have known. And nothing could have survived the attack. We've had a report from Berge.'

'I wonder,' Sampson said, half to himself. He looked down at the photograph in the folder.

'Yeoman must never know the truth, of course.'

'No,' agreed the silver-haired man. 'He must never know the truth.'

He reached out and took the folder from in front of Sampson, stared at it for a moment, then rose and locked it away in the bottom drawer of a steel cabinet.

The file on Madeleine Lefèvre was closed.

THE END

# A SELECTED LIST OF CORGI TITLES

WHILE EVERY EFFORT IS MADE TO KEEP PRICES LOW, IT IS SOMETIMES
NECESSARY TO INCREASE PRICES AT SHORT NOTICE. CORGI BOOKS RESERVE THE
RIGHT TO SHOW AND CHARGE NEW RETAIL PRICES ON COVERS WHICH MAY
DIFFER FROM THOSE ADVERTISED IN THE TEXT OR ELSEWHERE.

THE PRICES SHOWN BELOW WERE CORRECT AT THE TIME OF GOING TO PRESS

| | | | |
|---|---|---|---|
| ☐ 11307 7 | THE FIGHT OF THE FEW | | *Richard Hough* £1.25 |
| ☐ 11094 9 | ANGELS ONE-FIVE | | *Richard Hough* 85p |
| ☐ 11662 9 | THE BLOOD ORDER | | *Jack D. Hunter* £1.25 |
| ☐ 11672 6 | THE BLUE MAX | | *Jack D. Hunter* £1.25 |
| ☐ 11557 6 | TARGET TOBRUK | | *Robert Jackson* £1.00 |
| ☐ 11987 3 | MOSQUITO SQUADRON | | *Robert Jackson* £1.25 |
| ☐ 11231 3 | SQUADRON SCRAMBLE | | *Robert Jackson* 80p |
| ☐ 11195 3 | HURRICANE SQUADRON | | *Robert Jackson* 85p |
| ☐ 10783 2 | FIGHTER ACES OF WORLD WAR II | | *Robert Jackson* 70p |
| ☐ 11697 1 | THE WAR GOD | | *Frederick E. Smith* £1.50 |
| ☐ 11824 9 | 633 SQUADRON: OPERATION COBRA | | *Frederick E. Smith* £1.35 |
| ☐ 11075 2 | 633 SQUADRON: OPERATION VALKYRIE | | *Frederick E. Smith* £1.50 |
| ☐ 10741 7 | 633 SQUADRON: OPERATION CRUCIBLE | | *Frederick E. Smith* 80p |
| ☐ 10155 9 | 633 SQUADRON: OPERATION RHINE MAIDEN | | *Frederick E. Smith* £1.95 |
| ☐ 08169 8 | 633 SQUADRON | | *Frederick E. Smith* £1.25 |
| ☐ 11784 6 | A KILLING FOR THE HAWKS | | *Frederick E. Smith* £1.50 |
| ☐ 12026 X | JOHNNY KINSMAN | | *John Watson* £1.75 |

*All these books are available at your book shop or newsagent, or can be ordered direct from the
publisher. Just tick the titles you want and fill in the form below.*

**CORGI BOOKS**, Cash Sales Department, P.O. Box 11, Falmouth, Cornwall.

Please send cheque or postal order, no currency.

Please allow cost of book(s) plus the following for postage and packing:

**U.K. Customers** – Allow 45p for the first book, 20p for the second book and 14p for each
additional book ordered, to a maximum charge of £1.63.

**B.F.P.O. and Eire** – Allow 45p for the first book, 20p for the second book plus 14p per copy for
the next 7 books, thereafter 8p per book.

**Overseas Customers** – Allow 75p for the first book and 21p per copy for each additional book.

NAME (Block Letters) .................................................................................................

ADDRESS ....................................................................................................................

...................................................................................................................................